MANDIE
AND THE
JUMPING
JUNIPER

Mandie Mysteries

MANDIE
AND THE
JUMPING
JUNIPER

Lois Gladys Leppard

BETHANY HOUSE PUBLISHERS
MINNEAPOLIS, MINNESOTA 55438

Mandie and the Jumping Juniper
Lois Gladys Leppard

Library of Congress Catalog Card Number 91-73567

ISBN 1-55661-200-1

Published by Bethany House Publishers
A Ministry of Bethany Fellowship, Inc.
6820 Auto Club Road, Minneapolis, Minnesota 55438

Printed in the United States of America

The name of the character Mandie™ has been applied for as
a registered trademark.

To
Ingerlisa Wubbels
With Love

About the Author

LOIS GLADYS LEPPARD has been a Federal Civil Service employee in various countries around the world. She makes her home in Greenville, South Carolina.

The stories of her own mother's childhood are the basis for many of the incidents incorporated in this series.

Contents

"Thou shalt not go up and down as a talebearer among thy people. . . ."

Leviticus 19:16

Chapter 1 / Lost in the German Mountains

The carriage bounced along as the horses led it down the mountainous road in Germany. Mandie, Celia and Jonathan held to each other now and then to keep from sliding off their long seat. Mrs. Taft, Mandie's grandmother, and Senator Morton sat talking on the other seat, seemingly unaware of the jolts and unusual speed. Snowball, Mandie's white kitten, was safely snuggled between his mistress and the side of the carriage.

"These horses sure do fly!" Mandie said over the noise of the crunching gravel under the wheels. "Especially going downhill."

"Everyone drives fast in Germany," Jonathan told her. He had visited the country before.

"I'm anxious to see the castle where we're going to be staying, but I wish the driver would slow the horses down a little," Celia remarked as the shaking carriage jarred her words. She was sitting in the middle between Mandie and Jonathan.

Mandie leaned toward her two friends and said in a low voice, "I know Grandmother told the driver to hurry because she wanted to get to the Baroness's castle before dark, but I think the man is overdoing it."

Her friends nodded in silent agreement.

It was summertime in 1901. A tour of Europe was part of the education of all young people whose families could afford it. Mrs. Taft had brought thirteen-year-old Mandie and her friend Celia Hamilton to Europe while their school was recessed for the summer. Senator Morton, an old family friend, had come along.

Jonathan Guyer was supposed to be visiting relatives in Paris, but they weren't home when the group had visited that city. Therefore, he had traveled on with them under the care of Senator Morton, who was a friend of his father.

Mandie and the others had sailed to England from the United States. From there they had gone to Paris, on to Rome, and then to Switzerland. Now they were on their way to visit the Baroness Geissler, whom they had met in Rome. She had invited them to stay in her castle while in Germany.

Mandie, one hand grasping the passenger rope by the window, glanced outside in time to see a sharp curve descending steeply before them. She squeezed Celia's right hand tighter, causing Celia to grab Jonathan's hand with her left. Mandie released her hold on the passenger rope and grasped her kitten by his red collar.

"Don't look out!" Mandie gasped, quickly closing her eyes.

Mrs. Taft and Senator Morton suddenly became aware of the speed at which they were traveling as the vehicle suddenly lurched with an ear-splitting screech and then seemed to float through the air. Everyone clutched at everyone else as the carriage flipped over on its side and landed with a loud crash.

Mandie had managed to hold on to Snowball. He was frightened and meowing loudly.

Ignoring her pain, she scrambled to her hands and knees to look for her grandmother while she still held on to Snowball. Mrs. Taft lay silently near an open window, a dislodged seat across her legs. Senator Morton, bright red blood flowing down his cheek from a cut on his forehead, was trying to lift the broken seat to free her.

"Grandmother!" Mandie cried, tears blinding her as she crawled to Mrs. Taft's side. "Grandmother! Please wake up!" Mandie ran a hand lightly over her grandmother's face.

Then she stopped to look around her. Jonathan was nowhere to be seen. "He must have been thrown out when the carriage turned over," she said, anxiously. Turning back to her grandmother, she saw that Senator Morton had managed to remove the seat and Mrs. Taft's eyelids fluttered.

"Grandmother!" Mandie cried. She touched her face again. This time her grandmother's eyes opened and she looked at Mandie in shock.

"What happened?" she asked as the senator helped her to sit up. Then she caught sight of the wreck they were sitting in. "Oh, dear!" Senator Morton wiped the blood from his face with his handkerchief and she quickly asked, "Are you all right?"

"Yes, I'm all right," Senator Morton said, patting the cut on his forehead with his handkerchief. "It's just a scratch. I think we'd better all get out of here before what's left of this vehicle slides down the mountain. Let me help you."

"Jonathan is missing!" Mandie announced as she

crawled to the open door. The carriage was lying on its side and Mandie had to pull herself up to get out. With Snowball in one arm she climbed out and Celia quickly followed. Mrs. Taft and the senator came out after them.

Mandie looked around. The sun had set and the light was growing dim. Debris was scattered all around the wrecked carriage. She spotted one of her bags far below. There was no sign of Jonathan—and the driver of the carriage, where was he?

Mrs. Taft spoke behind her, showing her obvious frustration, "Where is that driver? He has completely ruined everything. Just look at our belongings scattered all over the mountainside."

"The horses are gone, too," Senator Morton said. "Evidently they broke loose when the carriage turned over."

There was a sudden rustling sound uphill from where they were standing. Mandie looked up to see Jonathan waving at them as he tried to make his way down the steep, rocky slope.

"Jonathan!" Mandie called to him. "I'm so glad you're all right!"

"I see the driver now," Senator Morton said as he looked below.

The others turned as the driver slowly made his way up to them.

"I hope he has a good explanation for what has happened. We could have been killed," Mrs. Taft said, turning to the girls. "Are you sure y'all are all right?"

Mandie tied Snowball's leash to a nearby bush and put him down. "I'm all right, I guess, but pretty dirty," Mandie said, brushing her rumpled traveling suit. She straightened her bonnet and tucked the stray wisps of blonde hair inside.

"I think I have a few scratches, but nothing serious,"

Celia said. She also began brushing at her clothes, but suddenly withdrew her left hand. "Oh! That hurt!" She rubbed her hand gingerly.

"Let me see, dear," Mrs. Taft said, moving slowly over the rocks to reach Celia. She examined the hand and Celia winced at her touch. "I don't believe any bones are broken, but you may have a bad sprain. We'll need to put it in a sling so you won't strain it further. Here, let's use this." Mrs. Taft removed the flowered silk scarf from her neck and placed it around Celia's, tying it in a knot, and then placing Celia's hand inside. "There, dear. We'll have a doctor look at it just as soon as we can get to one."

"Thank you, Mrs. Taft," Celia said, trying to smile.

Jonathan reached them a few seconds before the driver.

"How did you get up there?" Mandie asked.

"When I saw the carriage was going to flip, I jumped out," Jonathan told her.

"You're lucky you didn't break anything," Senator Morton said.

"Only a few scratches and bruises," the boy said, smiling mischievously as he patted his knees.

The driver finally made it up the steep incline. He was huffing and puffing as he spoke, "I am sorry for what happened, madam, sir," he said with a British accent as he stood sheepishly before Mrs. Taft and Senator Morton. "With your permission I will go seek help."

"From where?" Mrs. Taft demanded. "We're in the middle of the mountains! You should have been more careful. Our belongings are strewn all over the mountainside and are no doubt ruined. We are all bruised, scratched and cut. How could you have been so careless?" she scolded.

"I apologize, madam," the man said, not meeting her

eyes. "You had given me orders to hurry, and I was only trying to do what you asked."

"Oh, but I didn't mean to absolutely fly! You could have hurried at a safer speed," Mrs. Taft replied.

"If we had gone slower we would not have reached your destination before midnight," the man said. "But please understand that I am greatly distressed with what has happened. Now I will go down the road to look for help. I have never been on this route before, and I have no idea how far I will have to go, but I will return just as soon as possible."

As he turned to go, Mandie noticed that he was limping. He had probably injured his leg in the accident.

"Are you hurt?" she asked, anxiously.

"No, miss, not really, thank you," he replied.

"I am sorry you have to walk," Senator Morton spoke up. "I would volunteer to go with you, but I suppose it's best I stay here with the ladies."

"Yes," the man agreed with a nod as he walked on down the rough road.

"Now, there's no telling when he'll be back. We may have a long wait," Mrs. Taft remarked, assessing their helpless situation.

"While we wait, Jonathan, why don't you and I gather up our belongings?" Senator Morton suggested as he pulled the broken seat out of the carriage and set it down. "Mrs. Taft, maybe you'd like to rest here."

Mrs. Taft looked at him with a smile, adjusted her skirts and sat down. "Thank you, Senator Morton, that was thoughtful of you."

"I'll help you," Mandie told the senator as she followed him down the trail.

"I will, too," Celia added.

"No, Celia," Mandie ordered. "Remember, you have

only one good hand. You can stay here and keep an eye on Snowball. That would help."

"Well, all right," Celia replied, turning back. The white kitten was playing around the loose rocks at the end of his leash. Celia sat down on a large boulder near him and watched.

"Senator Morton, sir, why don't you gather the things nearby, and I'll do the climbing up and down the hill necessary to get the rest?" Jonathan offered.

Senator Morton stopped, looked at him with a smile and said, "You're right. I'm not as young as I used to be. You be careful though."

"Yes, sir," Jonathan replied, and turning to Mandie, said, "You get the small items and I'll get the heavier ones."

"But that's a trunk down there. I'll help you carry it," Mandie said, pointing downhill.

Jonathan looked at the trunk. "It does look pretty big. All right, let's go." He took her hand as they made their way down the mountainside.

Fortunately, Mandie had worn her everyday shoes because the dressy ones were not comfortable. She would never have been able to walk over this rough terrain with the heels on her newer ones.

"This sure was a terrible thing to happen," Mandie murmured as they carefully made their way down the rough slope. "But, you know, we're awfully lucky that no one was seriously hurt."

"When I felt the carriage about to turn over, I just knew we'd end up in a pile, that's why I jumped out," Jonathan repeated.

"It was all so sudden, I don't even know exactly what happened," Mandie said, shaking her head.

"A rear wheel broke," Jonathan told her. "I was in a

carriage once before when that happened, but we were going at a much slower speed so it didn't turn over. And no one was injured."

As they approached the trunk, Mandie said, "This is my grandmother's trunk. Thank goodness it didn't burst open."

They each grasped a leather handle, and Jonathan lifted one end of the trunk. Mandie could barely get the other end off the ground.

"Whew! This is going to be slow going," she gasped as she tightened her grip on the handle.

Jonathan straightened up to look around. "I think if we got this thing out onto the trail it would be easier to go uphill with it."

Mandie followed his gaze. A trail meandered around rocks and shrubbery, rather than going straight up to where the others waited, but it would be safer than climbing over the uncleared area.

"You're right," she agreed. "I know Grandmother is probably watching us, and we'll be out of her sight on that curve, but let's try it."

"If I lift my end too high it will throw the weight on you, so I'll try to keep it level with yours," Jonathan explained as they carried the trunk a few steps and then stopped to let Mandie flex her hand.

After they got onto the smoother dirt of the trail, Mandie didn't have to watch her feet so closely. At one point when they paused, Mandie exclaimed, "I see my bag over there! I'll come back for it."

"And there's mine," Jonathan said, motioning toward the other side of the trail.

When they finally reached the wrecked carriage, Senator Morton had recovered all the small items, so Mandie and Jonathan went back down to retrieve their bags.

Coming back up, Mandie told Jonathan, "I'm glad your aunt and uncle weren't home when we got to Paris, so you could come on the rest of the trip with us." She looked up at the dark-haired boy and smiled.

"I am, too," Jonathan replied. "I'm sure we're having a lot more interesting time, what with carriage wrecks, thieves in Rome, that mystery in Switzerland, and all the other things we've been involved in." He laughed and swung his bag in the air. "My aunt and uncle will never believe any of this when we finally catch up with them."

"Your father may catch up with us first," Mandie reminded him.

"He never has let Senator Morton know exactly what his plans are, so I'd guess that we'll be back in Paris before he turns up," Jonathan said.

"But we have lots more traveling to do yet," Mandie said, switching her bag to the other hand as they climbed the hill.

Celia stood up as the two reached the spot where the others were waiting. She extended her good hand for Mandie's bag, and said, "Mandie, I feel so useless, letting you and Jonathan do all the work." She set the bag down near the rest of the luggage.

"No, Celia, you are far from useless," Mandie assured her as she caught her breath. "You watched Snowball, and that can be quite a job sometimes." She bent to tickle the kitten under his chin. He stood up on his hind feet, meowing to be picked up. "You see, he's spoiled rotten, wanting me to pick him up after I've traipsed down the mountainside twice." She laughed and picked up the kitten, then sat on a rock to rest.

Mrs. Taft and Senator Morton were talking quietly nearby, and the young people listened.

"I am just about at the end of my rope," Mandie's

grandmother complained. "If that man doesn't come back with help soon, it's going to be dark as pitch out here in these mountains, and I'm already feeling cold."

Senator Morton quickly stood up and reached for a bag nearby. "I believe your cloak is in this bag. Let me get it for you." He pulled out the heavy brown garment and draped it around her shoulders.

"Oh, thank you, Senator," Mrs. Taft said, pulling the cape more tightly around her. "This is much better. I don't mean to complain, but I have never been in such a predicament where I have felt so helpless to do anything."

"I know what you mean," Senator Morton agreed. "If the driver doesn't return soon, perhaps I should go looking for help."

"Why, Senator, I'd be frightened to death without you here to protect us," Mrs. Taft said. "There's no telling who might come down that road."

Mandie held her breath to keep from giggling. Her grandmother knew just what to say to impress the senator. She looked at her friends and found them grinning, too.

Darkness covered the mountainside now, and the young people also pulled out their wraps against the cooler night air. Celia huddled near Mandie. Mandie looked at her friend by the moonlight, and realized her hand must be hurting. She put her arm around Celia and held Snowball tightly in her lap.

"Is there anything I can do to make your hand feel better?" Mandie asked her.

"No, I don't think so, Mandie," Celia said in a low voice. "I've had a sprain before. It just has to work itself out. I'll be all right."

"Are you sure?" Jonathan asked.

"Yes, I'm sure," Celia said, taking a deep breath. "Let's

talk about something else, if y'all don't mind."

"Like what the baroness will be thinking when we don't arrive on schedule?" Jonathan asked with a laugh.

"Maybe she'll send someone to look for us," Mandie said hopefully.

"I don't think so. She won't know we've had a wreck," Jonathan said.

"She might think we got lost," Celia said.

"And if she thinks that, she might send someone to look for us," Mandie reasoned.

"Maybe that driver will be back soon with another carriage," Jonathan said.

"If only Uncle Ned had come with us," Mandie mused. "He'd know what to do. He always does."

Uncle Ned was her father's old Cherokee friend, and when her father died the Indian had promised to watch over Mandie. He had been true to his promise. But at this particular time he had gone on horseback by a different route in order to stop and visit a friend whom he had known in the United States, and who was now in Germany on business. Uncle Ned planned to catch up with them at the castle. The exact time of his arrival there was uncertain.

"Amanda, y'all be sure you keep your wraps on," Mrs. Taft called. "I don't want any of you to catch cold."

"We could build a fire like the Indians do back home, Grandmother," Mandie suggested.

"No, we'd better not do that. It could get out of control," Mrs. Taft said.

"The driver will probably come back soon now," Senator Morton said, trying to encourage them.

"Seems like he's been gone an awfully long time. You'd think he would have met up with someone by now," Mandie said, shifting her sleeping kitten in her lap.

Suddenly Snowball woke up. He bristled his fur and stood.

"Snowball sees or hears something!" Mandie remarked, watching her kitten.

"Probably some wild animal," Jonathan said.

As the young people listened they heard a faint sound in the distance.

"It's a horse!" Celia said, rising excitedly.

"You're right," Mandie agreed. She stood and put Snowball down on his leash.

"Only one horse. Listen," Jonathan said.

The clopping sound was closer. Mrs. Taft and Senator Morton were standing now and looking too.

Everyone watched the road for any sign of help. Snowball growled at the end of his leash as a large dog trotted down the road and a lone horseman came slowly behind him.

Mandie strained in the darkness to see if it might be the carriage driver or, miracle of miracles, Uncle Ned. As the horse drew nearer she knew it couldn't be Uncle Ned. The rider was too small. He didn't look like the driver either. But whoever he was, maybe he would get them some help.

Quickly handing Snowball's leash to Jonathan, Mandie said, "I'm going to see who it is."

Jonathan tied the leash to a bush and joined her.

Celia stayed by the kitten, and Mrs. Taft and Senator Morton stood watching.

Mandie reached the edge of the road with Jonathan right behind her just as the rider came by. The dog spotted the two and barked viciously.

The rider drew up his horse. When he did, the dog backed up against the horse's legs and stopped barking.

"Mister, can you help us?" Mandie called to the man.

She was afraid to go any closer.

"Sprechen Sie Englisch?" Jonathan asked loudly.

"Nein, Nein!" came the quick, harsh reply as the rider leaned forward to peer at them.

"What did you say to him?" Mandie whispered.

"I only asked if he spoke English and he said 'no,'" Jonathan explained.

"He sounds awfully upset about something," Mandie said softly.

The rider began yelling and talking in a language that Jonathan could not understand. Senator Morton and Mrs. Taft, who had come over to see what was going on, could not understand either.

"I don't recognize the language," the senator said.

"Neither do I, but then I can't hear him very well," Mrs. Taft said. "His voice is muffled."

"Yes," the senator agreed.

Jonathan tried speaking to the man in French, but he either ignored him or couldn't understand. Suddenly he stood up in the stirrups and fired a gun in the air, then went racing off down the steep road, the dog running after him.

The group stood looking blankly at one another while the shot echoed away in the distance.

"That man was either crazy, drunk, or scared," Jonathan declared.

Mandie turned toward where they'd been sitting, and found Celia right behind her.

"I had to see what was going on," Celia whispered.

"I don't believe anybody knows what was going on," Mandie said.

"Well, it wasn't the driver. That's for sure," Jonathan said as he joined the girls.

"Amanda," Mrs. Taft spoke to her, "I think it's best if

you do not rush up to strangers like that again, especially in the dark. It could be dangerous."

"Yes, Grandmother. I just thought maybe it was someone who could help us," Mandie said. She picked up Snowball and hugged him close.

Senator Morton cleared his throat and announced his decision: "We can't stay out here all night. If that driver doesn't come back within the hour, I will go look for help myself."

"I'll go with you," Mandie volunteered.

"Amanda!" Mrs. Taft reproved her.

"But, Grandmother, a person should never go off alone in a strange place," Mandie countered.

"You wouldn't be of much help in an emergency," her grandmother said.

"I will go with you, Senator Morton," Jonathan offered.

"No, Jonathan. One of us needs to stay here with the ladies—to protect them," Senator Morton said.

"Well—" Jonathan began.

Mandie interrupted, "You see, Grandmother. I'm the only logical one to go with Senator Morton. Celia has hurt her hand, and Jonathan must stay here to protect you. That leaves me to go."

"Senator Morton hasn't asked you to go and besides, he hasn't decided for sure that he will go," Mrs. Taft said.

"I'll wait a little while longer, and if the man doesn't return we'll go," the senator said. "That is, if Amanda insists, and you agree, Mrs. Taft. It will be fine with me if she goes."

"All right, but you're not to leave Senator Morton's side. Is that understood?" Mrs. Taft asked sternly.

"Yes, Grandmother, I understand," Mandie quickly replied. "Thank you, Grandmother."

When the driver did not return within the hour, Mandie

left her kitten with her friends, and she and the senator set out down the road. The night became lighter as the full moon appeared from behind the trees, but as they walked on, the road became rougher.

Suddenly the moonlight was obliterated by a dense forest through which the road passed. There was no other way to go but through the forest.

Chapter 2 / Silent Help

Senator Morton slowed his steps and looked ahead. Mandie stayed right by his side.

"I do hope there's light enough to find our way through all those trees," he said.

"I've been through lots of forests, Senator Morton, back home in Swain County," Mandie told him. "After you get inside, your eyes adjust to the darkness. Then you can see all the night creatures, the owls, and the birds sleeping, and the crickets jumping all around."

"Yes, you're right, my dear," the senator said, looking down at her. "But you must remember to stay close to me. I don't want to lose you."

"I will, Senator Morton," Mandie promised. "I don't want to lose you either." She smiled up at the tall man as they walked on through the forest.

Mandie looked around, listening for the usual sounds she knew from the woods back home. She couldn't hear a single creature. She held her skirts close to keep from snagging them on the bushes along the way, and stayed as close by the senator's side as possible, until the road became too narrow for two people to walk abreast.

Senator Morton put a hand on Mandie's shoulder. "Wait, dear," he said. "This so-called road has turned into a mere pathway that would never accommodate anything as large as a carriage. Either we missed a turn somewhere or the road has run out."

"The driver said he had never been on this route before," Mandie said, trying to see ahead of them in the darkness. "Maybe this isn't the right road. I mean, maybe the driver didn't know how to get to the castle at all."

"That could very well be," Senator Morton agreed. "I wonder if we should go back to the wreck and go in the opposite direction."

"It'd be a long walk before we'd find anyone," Mandie reminded him. "Remember, it was all mountains the way we came, and no sign of anyone or any dwelling after we stopped at that inn to eat today."

"Yes, the road did seem to be deserted, but then your grandmother and I were busy talking and I didn't really notice," Senator Morton replied.

"Since we've already come this far, why don't we just see what's beyond this forest?" Mandie suggested.

"This could be a huge stand of trees," Senator Morton said.

"You know, I just realized something," Mandie said, looking up at him in the darkness. "That man on the horse came this way. There must be something beyond these woods."

"I don't think we want to meet up with that man again," Senator Morton said. "However, as you say, he had to be going somewhere. I suppose we could go a little farther."

"Good idea," Mandie quickly agreed.

Mandie walked in front of the senator on the narrow path. As they moved along slowly, silently, she kept listening. The only sounds were their own movements, the rustle of leaves as they brushed by them, and the crack of twigs beneath their feet.

There was a moldy odor. The forest was damp, with lots of dead underbrush.

After what seemed an awfully long time to Mandie, Senator Morton finally spoke.

"Wait," he said. "This must go on for miles and miles. And the path is so winding we may never find our way back if we keep going. Besides, if we do find someone to ask for help, how will we ever explain where the others are?"

"I can find the way back," Mandie told him. "I'm one-fourth Cherokee, remember? And Uncle Ned taught me how to mark a trail. If you want me to, I'll just start breaking twigs to show the way we've come." She let go of her long skirts and reached out to bend a twig on a bush. When it cracked she left it dangling. Senator Morton stood watching her, fascinated.

"Now how do you propose to find the bent twigs on the way back in this darkness?" he asked.

"Oh, that's easy," Mandie said. "You see, you bend twigs on the same side of the path all the way, and at the same height. Then all you have to do is look along the same line as you trace them back."

"Oh, I see, but what if you don't find bushes the same height down the path? Or you run out of bushes altogether?" he asked.

Mandie picked up a stick in the pathway and bent to make a mark in the dirt. "Then you mark the trail this way," she explained, making a crude arrow design.

"That sounds reasonable enough," Senator Morton said.

"Well, are we going ahead now?" she asked, straightening up to catch his response.

"If you think you can find the way back," the senator replied with a big smile.

"I can assure you we won't get lost!" Mandie said, turning to walk ahead.

An opening in the forest came before they knew it. The moon had disappeared though, and they found themselves in darkness almost equal to the deep forest.

"Well, we made it through," Mandie said, looking up at the clouded sky.

"Yes, and I do believe it's going to rain," the senator said.

They stood there surveying the situation. There was no sign of anyone or any dwelling, but the open space seemed to go on for miles. And the pathway they had been following intersected with a wide road.

"Look!" Mandie said, pointing to the road crossing in front of them. "Now which way do we go?"

Senator Morton went ahead to inspect the road and Mandie followed. "I'd say this is a well-traveled highway," he determined. "And since we are supposed to be journeying north, the direction to the castle should be to the right."

"Are we going all the way to the castle by ourselves?" Mandie asked.

"Not if we can find help before we get that far," the senator said. "And there should be somebody on this road. Let's go."

Even though they had made it through the forest, Mandie was tired and just couldn't get up much speed. After all, her legs weren't as long as the senator's.

"I think I see some boulders over there." The senator pointed to the left of the roadway. "Let's sit for a few minutes and catch our breath."

"Thanks," Mandie said. "I hope I'm not slowing you down."

"Why no, of course not," Senator Morton said with a smile as he sat down. "These legs of mine aren't as young as yours. I get tired too."

"But mine aren't as long as yours, so we're even," Mandie said, laughing.

They had hardly sat down when the sky seemed to open up and drenched them with a heavy downpour.

"Shall we go back to the woods for shelter?" Senator Morton asked as he turned up the collar of his coat.

"Oh, no, I won't melt, if you won't," Mandie said, pulling her cloak tighter around her. "Let's just get going. We might be real close to some place where we can get in out of the rain."

Senator Morton got up and shook the rainwater off his hat, then replaced it on his white hair.

"I hope your grandmother and the others can find some protection from this sudden downpour," he said as they started walking down the road.

"I do, too. We'll never hear the last of it if my grandmother's bonnet gets ruined," Mandie said with a laugh. "Especially after all the damage to our things in the accident. And I'm not sure they will be able to shelter our luggage from the rain."

"That was such a devastating thing," the senator replied. "We have to be thankful no one was killed or seriously hurt."

Mandie suddenly started jumping up and down and pointing down the road ahead of them. "I see a light! A light!" she cried, excitedly.

"Yes, I see it too. Just ahead," the senator said.

"Thank the Lord!" Mandie said, hurrying ahead despite the downpour. Her cloak was wet and heavy, slowing her progress. She reached down and gathered the skirt of it up into her arms.

Senator Morton followed closely. As they neared the light, Mandie could see that it was inside a small building. She breathed a sigh of relief. There must be someone there and maybe they would have a vehicle of some kind that could take them to Baroness Geissler's castle.

When they finally reached the dwelling, the rain suddenly stopped. Mandie turned to smile at Senator Morton and then started toward the door.

She dropped the skirt of her cloak and tried to shake out some of the water as she knocked. She could hear someone moving about inside but no one answered. She knocked again.

"I can hear someone in there, but they won't come to the door," she told Senator Morton.

"Yes, I can hear someone, too. Here, let me try," he said, stepping up and knocking heavily on the door. "Anyone home? Is there anyone home?" he called through the door.

The noise inside continued, but there was no response.

"I'll see if I can look through a window," Mandie suggested, stepping off the tiny stoop and going around the side of the hut.

She pressed her face close to the glass and could see an old man inside. He was replenishing the fire in his iron stove. She knocked on the glass but he didn't turn to look. As she watched she saw him put the last stick of wood in the stove. He turned to open a back door. She quickly ran around to the back.

Mandie gasped as the man opened the door and

looked at her. "Mister, can you help us? We've had a wreck."

The man looked at her in bewilderment without uttering a word.

"I believe the man's deaf," Senator Morton spoke up from behind her.

"Deaf? Oh, dear!" Mandie said. "What will we do now?"

"Let's try writing a note," Senator Morton suggested as he took a pad and pen from his pocket and quickly scribbled something on it. He held it out to the man, who was still staring at them.

The old man grunted, shook his head, and backed away.

"Maybe he doesn't understand English, Senator Morton. Why don't you try writing in German?" Mandie said.

"Of course," the senator said, writing again, this time in German. He extended the note to the man.

The man's face lit up and he reached for the note pad. He quickly wrote a reply and gave it back to Senator Morton. Then the man stepped back and motioned for them to come inside his house.

"I asked him if we could find a carriage or some conveyance to pick up your grandmother and your friends and go on to the castle," Senator Morton explained. "He wrote back that his name is Heider. He works for the baroness and this is her property. He will go to the castle for help while we stay here and dry out by his fire."

The senator wrote a thank you to the man who was hustling into a jacket and hat. He nodded, motioned for them to sit by his stove, and quickly left.

"At last!" Mandie sighed as she removed her wet cloak and sat on a low stool. "We'll soon be able to get Grandmother and Celia and Jonathan and go on to the castle!"

She took off her bonnet which had been covered by the hood of her cloak.

"Yes, and I'm afraid they're thinking we've gotten lost by now," Senator Morton said.

"The baroness must live in an isolated part of the country if this is her property. We haven't seen a single person or dwelling until now," Mandie remarked.

"I understand it's a huge estate," Senator Morton said. "However, Herr Heider—*Mr.* Heider—said he'd be back right away, so we must be close to the castle."

"Or the stables for the castle," Mandie added.

Even though Herr Heider did return shortly, the minutes seemed like hours to Mandie as she worried about her grandmother and her friends out there on that mountain road alone. And when she saw the huge elaborate carriage with a uniformed driver, Mandie clasped Herr Heider's hand and stood on tiptoe to plant a kiss on his cheek. He smiled and gave her a quick squeeze.

After they were seated inside the carriage, Senator Morton tried to explain to the driver where the others were. He didn't seem to understand. Mandie spoke up and told him it was through the woods and up a mountain. He smiled knowingly.

"But this carriage cannot get through the woods, so we go this way," the driver explained. He indicated the direction of the wide road they had walked. "Stupid driver you had, no one takes that road anymore. A big slide blocked it off years ago. But we find the others soon." He quickly closed the door and jumped up on his seat. Then he guided the thoroughbred horses swiftly down the road.

Even though they were traveling quite fast, Mandie noticed the luxurious carriage didn't bounce like the one they had rented earlier to carry them to the castle. Even so, she hoped this driver would slow down when he reached the rough road where they had had the wreck.

After a while it seemed to Mandie that they were going in circles, as the driver kept making left turns at various intersections. Finally she recognized the rough road they were searching for.

"This is it!" Mandie told the senator, excitedly. "Now we have to watch for the place where Grandmother and Jonathan and Celia are waiting."

"Yes, the driver said he would slow down on this road and look for them," Senator Morton assured her.

"At least the rain has stopped and the moon is back out," Mandie said, looking at the sky through the window, while watching for the others.

Their carriage suddenly stopped and the driver came back to speak to Senator Morton.

"I see a wrecked vehicle down there, but there are no people around here," he told him.

Mandie's heart beat faster. "Let me out. I want to see," she said, pushing at the door. The driver helped her down and Senator Morton followed.

They walked around the spot, calling the others' names without response.

"All the luggage is gone, too," Mandie said, as she came within sight of the place where she and Jonathan had piled it.

"It sure is," Senator Morton said.

"Look, what is that?" she asked, pointing toward the wrecked carriage. "Why it's an umbrella. It's open and just standing there."

"I do believe it belongs to Jonathan," Senator Morton said. "I can't imagine what happened, unless someone else gave them a ride."

Mandie spied a piece of paper under the shelter of

the umbrella. "Look, a note from Jonathan! It says: 'The driver sent another carriage for us and he will take us on to the castle. We know you will have some method of transportation when you return, so rather than be drowned out here in this downpour we are leaving. See you there.' Well, at least they got a ride." She handed the note to the senator.

The driver stood by listening and waiting. Senator Morton turned to him and said, "I suppose all we can do is return to the castle with you. The others should be there before we arrive."

"Yes, we will go now," the driver agreed.

Mandie snatched up the umbrella and closed it, bringing it along with her.

"They're probably dried out and have already eaten while we still slog around in these wet clothes," Mandie mumbled. Then she straightened up as they neared the waiting carriage and added, "But I'm really glad the driver sent another carriage after them. I know my grandmother must have been awfully worn out by then."

She looked at the senator as the driver closed their door.

"The only sad thing about it is, Jonathan and Celia don't get to ride in this great big fancy carriage!" she said with a smile.

"That's right," he agreed. "Well, at least the baroness didn't send her motor car for us."

"Oh, goodness, yes!" Mandie exclaimed. "I don't think I'll ride in that while we're here. That one ride in her car in Rome was enough for me!"

"But she has the latest and most expensive model out right now," Senator Morton said, smiling.

"You know me, Senator. I'm a country girl. I love riding in carriages with horses. It's safer," Mandie said, quite seriously.

"Safer? But what about the wreck we had today?" he asked.

"That was just plain carelessness on the part of the driver," Mandie replied.

"Yes, I agree with you," Senator Morton said. "But one of these days, and soon I predict, we'll be replacing carriages with motor cars."

"Not me. If I live to be a hundred I will keep a carriage." She glanced out the window and said, "Look, isn't that Herr Heider's house?"

"It's almost too dark to tell, but I believe it is," Senator Morton acknowledged.

"Then we are nearing the castle," Mandie said. "I do hope the baroness has a lot of good hot food waiting and a nice warm bed." She sighed with fatigue.

The driver followed a long, winding, tree-lined road to a huge stone building. As they circled the place, Mandie cried out in excitement when she spotted a real drawbridge let down over a creek on one side. However, the carriage didn't go inside by that way, as she expected from the stories she had read about castles in the old days. Instead, the driver brought it to a halt in front of a huge doorway, so wide that the vehicle could easily have gone through it.

As the driver jumped down and opened their door, a uniformed butler appeared in the doorway of the building and stood waiting for them to come up the steps. He spoke to them in perfect British English.

"The baroness bids you welcome. She is not presently at home but she will return shortly. The housekeeper will get you settled," he said in a very businesslike manner.

Mandie looked up at the tall, slender man. Though he was bald, she thought he would have been handsome if he had just smiled at her.

"Are my grandmother and my friends here yet?" she asked as they paused on the steps.

"No one else has arrived. Is the baroness expecting more guests?" the man asked.

"Yes, my grandmother, Mrs. Taft, and my friends, Jonathan Guyer and Celia Hamilton. We were all invited," Mandie replied.

"I am sorry. No one else has arrived," he repeated. "Were you not all together?"

"Yes, we were," Senator Morton spoke up. "We had an accident and your driver picked us up at Herr Heider's house where we had gone for help. When we went back to get the others they were gone, leaving a note to the effect that someone had come for them."

The driver of the baroness's carriage had been standing in the yard listening to the conversation and now he said, "Perhaps they have not had time. I know the shorter way."

"You're probably right," Mandie agreed.

An older woman in a crisp uniform came out to stand behind the butler. "If you will come with me," she said. "My name is Jahn and I am the housekeeper of the baroness. This way, please."

She led them inside through several jumbled passageways with stone floors and big woooden doors to various rooms. Finally they came to some narrow stone steps.

"You will occupy the rooms on the next floor," she informed them, and hurried on ahead up the stairs.

"I can't imagine my grandmother going up and down steps like these, so steep and narrow and not even a handrail to hold on to," Mandie remarked to the senator as they followed the housekeeper.

Frau Jahn heard the remark and turned back to tell

them, "Oh, but there are other stairs with handrails. These are only the first we happened to come to."

"That's good," Mandie replied. "I'm sure she'll prefer those with a rail."

The woman showed them rooms upstairs near the end of a long hallway. She pushed open one door and turned to the senator, "This one for you, sir." Stepping across the corridor she opened another door and spoke to Mandie, "And this one for you."

"Thank you," Mandie said as the senator also thanked the woman. Pausing in the doorway, she turned around to exclaim, "I forgot! We don't even have our luggage. We can't change out of these wet clothes until Grandmother and the others get here."

"Oh, well, at least we can wash up," Senator Morton said, turning to enter his room.

"I can find a robe for you, young lady," the house-keeper offered. "And if you will give me your wet clothes I will dry them for you."

"Oh, thank you," Mandie replied.

"And, sir, I can get something for you also if you wish to stay in your room," Frau Jahn said. "I will have the maid bring both of you some hot food. I'll be right back." She hurried down the hallway.

"I hope Grandmother gets here soon," Mandie said as she went into her room. "See you tomorrow morning, Senator."

"Yes, dear, I hope you sleep well," the senator replied as he closed the door to his room.

The housekeeper soon returned with a fancy silk robe that was a little big for Mandie, but it felt comfortable after the wet clothes. After Frau Jahn had taken her clothes away and the maid brought some food, Mandie curled up in a big chair in front of a roaring fire in the huge fireplace.

She was so tired she soon dozed off. A falling log in the fireplace woke her. She jerked upright and for a moment wondered where she was. The cuckoo clock on the mantelpiece "cuckooed" two o'clock in the morning.

"Goodness, Grandmother must not have gotten here yet," she said to herself. "Or somebody would have brought my luggage."

She rose and paced the floor, and finally decided to knock on the senator's door.

"Senator Morton, are you still up?" she called through the door.

"Yes, dear, I am," he replied, opening the door to his room. He was wearing somebody's workclothes.

"Has my grandmother gotten here yet?" Mandie asked.

"No, I don't believe so," he said.

"Shouldn't they have been here a long time ago?" she asked, anxiously.

"I would think so. In fact, I was wondering if I should go down and ask whether there has been any word from them," Senator Morton said with a frown.

"Please do, Senator Morton. I'm really worried," Mandie told him.

He went downstairs while Mandie waited in her room with the door open. When he returned he reported that the baroness kept various shifts of people working twenty-four hours, but the man he spoke to had not received any news. The baroness had come home some time ago, had waited up for her other guests, and finally gone to bed.

Mandie began pacing the floor again. *Where, oh, where could Grandmother, Jonathan, and Celia be?*

Chapter 3 / Together Again

Senator Morton stood in the open doorway to Mandie's room as they talked.

"What are we going to do?" Mandie asked. "Do you think they got lost? Or maybe had another accident?"

"I suppose we could borrow the carriage and recruit a driver to go look for them," the senator suggested. "There seem to be plenty of people working around this place, and I'm sure we could find someone, if not the driver who came and got us—"

Mandie hastily interrupted him, "Yes, please do, Senator Morton. If you will arrange it, I'll get dressed real fast." She turned back into the room and whirled around suddenly. "My clothes! The housekeeper took my clothes to dry them. Please, Senator Morton, could you find out where she took them? I don't have anything else to put on."

"Calm down, dear," he told her. "You wait here and I'll be right back with your clothes. I'll find them somehow.

And I'll also arrange for a driver and carriage."

Mandie left her door open to wait impatiently.

Maybe I shouldn't have come on this trip to Europe, she thought. The whole thing had been studded with disaster, everywhere they went. Right now she would like to be home in her own bed, with her mother and Uncle John nearby. Once they were all safely home again she didn't think she'd ever leave. She was just plumb tuckered out.

She flopped in the big chair by the fireplace, but bounced right up again. She couldn't sit still not knowing what was happening to her grandmother, Celia, and Jonathan.

Senator Morton tapped on the open door. Mandie turned to see him holding a dark cloak.

"I'm terribly sorry dear, but the maid on duty downstairs says Frau Jahn put your clothes and mine in a room that she keeps locked. She went to bed, and no one else has the key. However, the maid offered you her own cloak," he explained quickly.

"Our clothes are locked up? How silly! She knew we'd be needing them soon," Mandie said, unhappily.

"Yes, dear, but don't you understand? The house-keeper hung them to dry in a room where no one would bother them. She did it innocently enough," the senator said. "Here, let's see if this cloak will fit. The maid didn't look much bigger than you."

"All right. It's just that I'm upset about the others not arriving yet," Mandie said, quickly throwing the cloak over the robe she was wearing.

"It does fit all right, and I believe it's wool," Senator Morton commented, looking down at her stocking-feet. "You do have your shoes?"

"Oh, yes. They should be dry now. I've had them over

here by the fire," Mandie said, hurrying to the hearth. "Yes, they are dry." She quickly slipped her shoes on and buttoned them up.

As they walked down the long hallway together, Senator Morton said, "I was able to engage the same driver who brought us here. So that should simplify things a little. He will know the roads we took. His name is Kurt."

The driver had the carriage waiting for them at the door and he also had another man along in case they needed him. There were extra lanterns besides the usual ones on the carriage for night driving.

Mandie was delighted to find hot foot-warmers on the floor of the carriage and extra blankets on the seats. It was obvious the baroness had a well-run operation going in the castle. But remembering the lady whom she had met in Rome, Mandie was not surprised. There had been a definite air of authority about her, even though she didn't speak a word of English. Mandie had not been able to understand a thing the baroness said except through interpretation by her grandson, Rupert, who had been driving her motor car.

As they drove off into the dark night Mandie asked the senator, who sat on the opposite seat, "What are you planning to do? Where are we going?"

"Kurt and I discussed that, and we've decided to go back to the place where we had the accident and then come around the long way to the castle. Remember, he said he came by a short-cut when he brought us," Senator Morton explained.

"And what if we don't find them?" Mandie asked anxiously as she pulled the blanket around her.

"We'll find them somewhere," the senator assured her.

Mandie noticed he had put on somebody's heavy

woolen coat over the workclothes he was wearing. Even in the summertime it seemed awfully cold at night in the German mountains—and her worry added to the chill.

The driver drove slowly down the road so that they could all watch out for any sign of anyone along the way. This made Mandie nervous because she wanted to hurry up and find her grandmother and Celia and Jonathan, but she kept telling herself they might overlook something if they traveled too fast.

They met no other vehicles on the road and saw no one. As they approached the site of the wrecked carriage, the driver slowed down and stopped. He came to the door to speak to Senator Morton.

"I thought perhaps you might want to look around here again," Kurt said.

Senator Morton and Mandie were both already getting out of the carriage.

"Yes, yes, of course," Senator Morton agreed as he stepped down and gave Mandie his hand to assist her.

"But we've already looked around here," Mandie said, pulling the wool cloak around her tightly. She shivered in the night air.

The other man helped the driver with the lanterns and the group walked around the area. All they could see was the wrecked carriage and the debris.

"You know, we never did know what happened to the horses that were pulling our carriage," Mandie remarked.

"Since they didn't stay around, they must not have been injured, and simply ran away. You can see that the shafts are broken and also the leather thongs on the shafts are split apart." Kurt showed her with the aid of a lantern as he explained.

"At least they must have made a clean break," Mandie said, straightening up. She walked to the embankment that she and Jonathan had descended to retrieve the trunk. Swinging out the lantern the man had given her, Mandie leaned toward the edge to light up the rocks below. There was nothing to be seen except the rocks and bushes.

"Amanda, please be careful," Senator Morton cautioned her as she stood near the edge of the cliff.

Mandie quickly straightened up. "I will—" Then she gasped, and exclaimed, "Listen, Listen! I hear something!" She stood still.

The other two men were searching a distance away. Senator Morton came to her side.

"What is it, dear?" he asked.

"It's Snowball! It has to be! Don't you hear him?" she cried, whirling around. "He's down there!"

"Yes, it does sound like a cat," the senator agreed. "But I don't think your grandmother would have gone off and left Snowball here."

Mandie turned back to the edge and stooped down to cast the light further on the area below. She saw a tiny spot of white. "There he is! It *is* Snowball!" She stood up and turned around. "I've got to get him."

Senator Morton clasped her arm. "Wait, Amanda. You can't go climbing around those rocks in the dark, especially with that long cloak on. We'll get the men to go down there."

Mandie hesitated. "Snowball probably won't let the men pick him up. He doesn't know them. Besides, he may be hurt. I've got to get him myself," she insisted.

The senator held firmly to her arm. "No, Amanda, please be sensible about this. Let the men at least try."

"Well, all right," Mandie finally agreed. "I'll walk on down the trail and call to him while the men go down to get him."

By now the two men had come back, and after a quick explanation from Senator Morton they hurried down the steep incline toward where Mandie had pointed. And Mandie, holding up the skirts of the long cloak and the robe beneath it, slowly made her way down the rough trail.

"Snowball, where are you?" she called loudly. "Come here, Snowball! Kitty, Kitty!"

There was no sound from the kitten until she had gotten halfway down. Then a loud, angry meow met her ears. She was finally close enough to see him through the darkness. He was perched on top of a huge boulder with nothing close enough for him to jump to. He wouldn't even try to get down.

Mandie stopped on the trail as near as she could get to him and called out, "Snowball, jump down. Come here at once! Do you hear? Snowball!"

The white kitten began meowing loudly at the sound of his mistress's voice and began to circle the top of the rock. He stopped to peer at Mandie.

The two men had located the cat by now, and they surveyed the smooth sides of the boulder that was much taller than they were.

"We will throw a rope up to him, miss," Kurt called to Mandie. "If he sticks his claws in it we'll give a quick jerk and he'll fall right down into our arms."

"Oh, please, be careful," Mandie yelled back across the bank.

She watched as Kurt coiled a thin rope and tossed it up on the top of the boulder. Snowball backed off in fright and almost fell off the other side. Kurt pulled the rope back down.

"We will try again," Kurt called to Mandie.

She saw the rope hurl up again and this time she

called to the kitten, "Snowball, catch it! Snowball, catch the rope!" She had often played with him this way, and he always caught the rope or string without any trouble.

This time when the rope landed, Snowball moved backward and then crept slowly forward to smell it.

Everyone waited. Mandie held her breath and then called to him again, "Snowball, get the rope. Get it!"

Snowball finally sank his claws into it and pulled it toward him.

The men below quickly gave a tug and before Mandie could say another word her kitten was safely down in the arms of Kurt.

"Got him, miss!" he called to Mandie as he tried to hold on to the squirming kitten and start back up the bank.

When Mandie met the men at the top on the roadway where Senator Morton had been waiting and watching, Snowball was putting up an awful protest. Kurt held the kitten's feet together so he couldn't scratch.

"Snowball! Shame on you! You should be grateful to the man," Mandie told him as Kurt handed him to her.

"Is he all right?" Senator Morton asked as he bent to look.

Mandie quickly examined her pet. "I think he's all right," she said. "He's probably hungry and he's also wet from the rain." She straightened up to look at the senator. "But, Senator Morton, my grandmother would never go off and leave Snowball. How did this happen?"

"I don't know, dear, unless Snowball got lost and they couldn't find him," the senator said.

"Oh, Snowball, if you could only talk," Mandie said as she cuddled him close in the folds of the long cloak.

"Shall we go on?" Kurt asked.

"Yes, I think we'd better," Senator Morton told him.

"Take the long way back to the castle and we'll see if we can find anything on that road."

Kurt got the carriage turned around and they drove several miles back in the direction from which Mandie and her group had traveled the previous day. After a long time Kurt turned the vehicle onto a wide road, and here and there Mandie could make out small dwellings along the way. But there was no sign of anyone anywhere.

Finally they came to the road that Mandie knew led to the castle. By this time the sky was beginning to lighten with the first rays of the morning sun.

"Senator Morton, we didn't find a thing, except Snowball of course," Mandie said. "What are we going to do now?"

"Kurt and I discussed the possibility of not finding them, and decided we would go all the way back to the town where we rented the carriage that was wrecked yesterday," the senator said. "The note from Jonathan said our driver had sent someone else to get them. Therefore, the owners of the carriage should know something."

"Just give me time to round up my clothes and I'll go back with you," Mandie told him as Snowball stood up and turned around in her lap.

"I'll change too before we leave again," he said.

Kurt circled the castle as he had done when he first brought them there, and as Mandie watched out the carriage window, she saw another carriage standing in the driveway ahead. She couldn't believe her eyes when she saw her grandmother being assisted down from the vehicle by the driver, and her friends Celia and Jonathan scrambling out behind her.

Mandie reached for the door at the same time. "They're here!" she cried. "Look!"

Kurt had stopped their carriage and had come back

to open the door for them. Mandie in her haste threw the door open and almost knocked him down.

"Oh, I'm sorry!" she exclaimed as she stumbled down the steps. Kurt caught his balance and reached out to assist her.

"That's quite all right, miss. I know that must be your grandmother and friends," he said, smiling at her.

"Yes, it is!" Mandie cried as she ran toward her grandmother, who had just straightened up and turned toward her.

Mandie threw her arms around her grandmother, with Snowball in tow on his leash. "Oh, Grandmother, thank the Lord you're all right," she cried as tears streamed down her face.

"Yes, dear, in spite of our ordeal we're all here safely," Mrs. Taft said, returning the embrace. When she released Mandie she saw Snowball. "Where did you find him?"

"Snowball? Oh, Grandmother, I'm freezing. Let's go inside and I'll tell you what happened."

Mandie turned to her friends and smothered them with hugs too. Senator Morton assisted Mrs. Taft as they all entered the castle.

Even though it was barely daylight, Frau Jahn was at the door to greet them.

"You have had such an experience! Perhaps you'd like a cup of tea by the fire in the drawing room before you go upstairs?" Frau Jahn suggested.

Mrs. Taft hesitated, but Mandie quickly made up her mind for her.

"Please, Grandmother, while we are all together, let's talk about what happened," Mandie begged, still holding firmly to Snowball.

"I suppose we'd better, and then we can rest," Mrs. Taft agreed. She turned back to Frau Jahn and asked,

"What time does the baroness usually rise in the morning?"

"Much later, madam," the housekeeper told her. "Shall I show you to the drawing room now?"

"Yes, please," Mrs. Taft said.

They followed the housekeeper down several hallways and were shown into a drawing room decorated in deep red and gold, where a fire was blazing in an enormous fireplace.

Too exhausted to make much observation, Mandie followed the adults to the chairs by the fire, threw off the cloak she was wearing, and plopped down on a low settee. Celia and Jonathan joined her.

Snowball wanted down, and Frau Jahn noticed him for the first time.

"If you please, I will take the cat and ask the cook to feed him," she offered.

"Thank you," Mandie said, handing his leash to her. "But please, be careful that he doesn't get out. He has already been lost once. He likes to run away."

Frau Jahn took Snowball into her arms and cuddled him. The kitten seemed content.

"We will be careful, miss. He will be fed in a closed room where he cannot escape," she promised. "I will send the maid with tea immediately."

As soon as Frau Jahn left the room, everyone spoke at once. Mandie and her grandmother looked at each other and they both said, "Tell me—"

Mandie laughed, and said, "You first, Grandmother. *Where* have y'all been? We've been nearly worried to death!"

"Yes, and so have we," Mrs. Taft replied. "We left you a note."

"We got the note when we went back to look for you,

but that was a long time ago," Mandie told her. "What happened?"

"As the note said, our driver sent another carriage for us," Mrs. Taft began. "After we got all the luggage loaded onto it, we started out. The driver, like the first one, had never been in the area before and he thought he knew the way to the castle, but we had to backtrack on the road we had traveled earlier. Then after we were miles and miles down that road, Celia suddenly realized Snowball was missing."

"I'm sorry, Mandie," Celia said, squeezing her hand.

Mandie squeezed her hand back and said to her grandmother, "As you saw, we found Snowball, but I'll tell you about that when you're finished."

"Well, we turned around and went back to look for him. Jonathan and Celia searched the whole area and couldn't find him, so we decided we'd get on to the castle and have you go back later and look for him. You know sometimes he won't come to other people like he will to you," Mrs. Taft explained.

"You are right about that," Senator Morton said, smiling at Mrs. Taft.

"So when we started back, the driver somehow took the wrong road and we ended up in a village a long way off. By that time everyone was tired and worn out and confused," she continued.

A uniformed maid quietly brought tea on a cart and set everything out before Mrs. Taft. Everyone waited silently.

"Would you require anything else, madam?" the girl asked.

"No, thank you," Mrs. Taft replied and smiled, dismissing the maid.

As her grandmother reached for the teapot, Mandie

got up to help her. "I'll pass the tea," she offered.

Getting a good look at her granddaughter, Mrs. Taft gasped, "Amanda, what are you wearing?"

Mandie looked down at the borrowed robe, and said, "It's a robe the housekeeper gave me. My clothes were all wet and I didn't have anything to change into. Please continue, Grandmother."

Mrs. Taft cleared her throat and went on, "As I was saying, we were all tired and cross so I discharged the driver and carriage and rented another one in the village. This man knew where we wanted to go. He brought us here and here we are!"

Jonathan spoke up, "The first driver found the horses. They weren't too far away. The second driver told us he had brought them back."

"Now, dear, what happened to you and Senator Morton after you left us?" Mrs. Taft asked as she sipped the hot tea.

Mandie quickly related their experiences and then she finally remembered to ask, "Celia, how is your hand?"

Celia smiled and said, "It's going to be all right."

"Oh, dear, Celia, how awful of me," Mrs. Taft said. "I must get the maid to bring you some liniment for your wrist."

When the maid came to show them to their rooms, she returned at Mrs. Taft's request to get some medicine, and promised to bathe Celia's wrist for her.

Senator Morton took Mrs. Taft's arm and said, "You don't know how relieved I am to know that you are finally safely here."

"And so am I," she said, returning his smile.

The others were shown to their rooms, and Mandie was grateful that they were all located close together.

Mandie and Celia had adjoining rooms, and Mandie

sat by the fire with her friend while the maid bathed Celia's wrist. Snowball had also been brought back, and was now playing around the hearth.

"Thanks for putting us in rooms together," Mandie said. "We'll probably sleep together, since this is a strange place to us."

"This is indeed a strange place," the maid said as she rubbed Celia's wrist.

"What do you mean by that?" Celia asked.

"Strange things happen here sometimes, which no one can explain," the girl told her.

"Like what?" Mandie asked eagerly.

"Like that huge juniper tree that jumps up and down sometimes," the maid said.

"A juniper tree that jumps up and down? How could that be?" Mandie asked.

"No one knows yet, but it happened again last night," the girl said.

"I never heard of a tree that could jump!" Celia said in a nervous voice.

"This one is probably forty feet tall. It's an unbelievable sight, but it has been seen to jump up and down occasionally," the girl said. She replaced the stopper on the bottle of liniment. "I must go now. You young ladies get some sleep and I will bring you some food later."

"Thank you," Celia said.

"What is your name?" Mandie asked.

"No one told you? My name is Olga, and if you need anything please let me know," the girl said, smiling.

"A tree that jumps up and down? Do you believe that, Celia?" Mandie asked as they jumped into the big bed and Snowball followed to curl up on their feet.

"No, I don't, Mandie," Celia said. "I don't see how it could be possible."

"Well, we'll just find out whether she is making up tales or not," Mandie declared as they both drifted off to sleep.

Chapter 4 / The Dungeon

The girls felt as though they had just gone to sleep when Olga was waking them. She had brought them cups of hot tea.

"Your grandmother says you girls are to drink this tea, get dressed properly, and come down to the dining room for the noon meal," she told them all in one breath as she set the tray on a nearby table.

Mandie and Celia sprang upright, disoriented at first. Snowball jumped down off the bed and prowled around.

"Oh, I know what he's looking for," Mandie said, jumping out of bed to get the kitten. She turned to the maid, and asked, "You don't happen to have a sandbox for my kitten, do you?"

"A sandbox? You mean a box with sand in it?" the maid asked, puzzled by the American term.

"Yes, you know, a place where he can go to the bathroom," Mandie replied.

"Oh, that is no problem," she said, walking across the

room and opening a door. "Here is the bathroom."

Mandie, exasperated with the girl's lack of under-standing, and worried that Snowball might soil the carpet, said, "I know that is the bathroom. But my kitten needs his own little commode."

"Ah, yes, commode!" Olga exclaimed, understanding at last. She pushed the door open to the bathroom. "His commode is right here."

Mandie followed her and saw the pottery bowl full of sand at the end of the bathtub. She put Snowball on the floor, and he ran straight to the bowl and jumped up.

"Thank goodness!" she sighed, and followed the maid back out into her bedroom.

Celia was up and checking the luggage, which had been set in one corner of the room. They had taken night-clothes from their small overnight bags when they re-adied themselves for bed.

"Mandie, we haven't unpacked! What are we going to put on?" she asked.

"I'd forgotten. We'll probably find everything all tan-gled up inside our trunks after that tumble in the carriage yesterday," Mandie said, shaking her head.

"But that is my job," Olga said. "I will unpack your belongings and hang them up." She went straight to the trunks. "I did not know they were not done."

"That's because we only got our luggage early this morning when my grandmother and the others finally got here," Mandie explained. She opened her purse on the bureau and got her key while Celia did the same.

Celia had no trouble unlocking her trunk, but the lock on Mandie's seemed to have been damaged in the wreck. She couldn't get the key to turn. Neither could Olga.

"I will get a man to do this for us. He will be stronger," Olga said, straightening up. "As soon as you girls go downstairs he will come up."

"Thank you," Mandie said. "But what will I put on right now?"

"Mandie," Celia quickly offered, "my things are not damaged, only wrinkled. Maybe you can find something of mine to put on that won't look too bad."

"Well, if you don't mind, I sure would appreciate it," Mandie said, walking over to Celia's trunk. "What do you want me to wear?"

"Anything you like, Mandie. We are about the same size, so I think anything would fit you all right," Celia said. "Choose whatever you want."

"No, you tell me what," Mandie insisted. "What are you going to wear?"

Celia bent over to look, and picked up a dress from the top. "Oh, I suppose I'll put on this green one." She shook it out and hung it across the back of a chair.

Mandie picked up the next dress and said, "Then I'll just wear this blue one, if you don't mind." She held it up. "I'm sure it'll fit." She draped it across another chair. "I don't believe they'll be too wrinkled to wear."

"You girls drink your tea quickly and I will help you get dressed," Olga offered as she pulled more dresses out of Celia's trunk and spread them out on the bed.

While they dressed Mandie asked the maid, "Will you show us the juniper tree that jumps up and down?"

"The jumping juniper tree? Oh, yes, you passed it when you came here," Olga told her as she buttoned the back of Mandie's dress. "It stands right around the corner from the drawbridge."

"I was tired both times we came in and I don't really remember anything about the outside of this house. I saw the moat, but it was dark," Mandie explained as she turned to the mirror to brush her hair.

Olga helped Celia into her dress, and commented, "When you go outside look for it. It is the oldest tree here, I understand, and the tallest."

"And you say it really does jump up and down?" Mandie questioned her as she tied her long blonde tresses back with a ribbon.

"I have never seen it do so, but others have, and as I mentioned, it happened just last night after dark," Olga said, straightening the bow in Celia's sash.

"We'd better go, Mandie," Celia urged her friend.

Mandie looked in the mirror and decided Celia's dress did fit all right. It was a bit loose in the waist, and almost too long, but no one would know it wasn't hers.

"Yes, yes, we must go," Olga agreed. "I will take you to the dining room. Then I will get the man to open the trunk, so I can finish unpacking. I will bring food for your cat also."

"Thank you," the girls said at once.

As Olga ushered them into a large dining room, they found Mrs. Taft and Senator Morton sitting at opposite sides of a linen-covered table, with the Baroness Geissler seated at one end. The housekeeper stood nearby, and they soon learned she was acting as interpreter since the baroness could not speak English and Mrs. Taft could not speak German. Senator Morton had some knowledge of it but was not fluent.

The girls smiled at the baroness, and greeted Mrs. Taft and Senator Morton as Olga seated them, Celia by the senator and Mandie by her grandmother.

Frau Jahn spoke to the girls after the baroness said something in German to her, "The Baroness Geissler welcomes you to her home and hopes that you will have a comfortable, happy time here."

"Thank you," the girls said together as they smiled at

the baroness. Then Mandie asked Frau Jahn, "How do you say thanks in German?"

Frau Jahn smiled and said, "*Vielen Dank*." She pronounced it slowly, "FEEL-en DAHNK."

Mandie picked it up at once and repeated the words to the baroness, who beamed with pleasure, and then spoke to Frau Jahn in German again.

"The baroness says you have a talent for German, and that you must learn the language so you can converse with her," the housekeeper told Mandie.

"Thank you," Mandie said, repeating it in German. "And please tell the baroness that I will teach her English if she would like."

When the housekeeper told this to the baroness, she responded immediately, and Frau Jahn once more told Mandie what she had said. "The baroness says she is much too old to learn another language, but she will ask her grandson to teach you our language." She paused as someone entered the room.

Mandie turned to see Rupert and Jonathan.

"Here he is now."

The baroness spoke to her grandson in German, and he sat down next to Mandie. The housekeeper seated Jonathan by Celia.

"Good morning," Jonathan greeted everyone. "Sorry I overslept."

"Yes, good morning, everyone," Rupert added as the greetings were returned.

Rupert was a tall, robust young man with a rosy complexion and eyes almost as blue as Mandie's. He was a few years older than she.

Mandie remembered when she'd met him in Rome for the first time. He seemed snobbish then, but this morning he was the perfect gentleman. She noticed that he kept glancing at his grandmother, as if to see if she were looking. The baroness continued to speak in German, with Frau Jahn interpreting for Mrs. Taft and Senator Morton.

Mrs. Taft related their experiences in getting to the castle. The baroness was shocked.

The maids began serving the food, and the young people carried on their own conversation.

"Rupert, I hear you have a forty-foot juniper tree that jumps up and down," Mandie said casually to the young man. Celia listened from across the table. Glancing at Jonathan, Mandie remembered that he had not been present when Olga told them about the tree.

"A what?" Rupert said in surprise, and then added arrogantly, "Where did you hear such a stupid tale?"

Mandie decided instantly not to reveal her source and replied, "One of the people who works for you told us about it. Do you not know of it?"

Celia watched him closely. Jonathan looked from one to the other.

Rupert laid down his fork and turned to Mandie. "I can assure you there is no such thing on this estate. Now, I'd rather not hear tales someone has composed about our property." He picked up his fork and resumed eating.

Mandie looked at him in surprise and then at Celia. She couldn't hear her, but Celia was obviously explaining what they'd heard to Jonathan under her breath. He smiled mischievously at Mandie.

The young people finished the rest of their meal in silence. According to Frau Jahn's interpretation, the baroness was planning a dinner in their honor for the next night. Several hundred guests had been invited. *Hundreds?* Mandie wondered if the housekeeper had made a mistake. It was evident the castle was large enough to accommodate that many people for a meal, but did the baroness have that many friends?

Celia cleared her throat to get Mandie's attention. Then she smiled and rolled her eyes toward the adults. Mandie quickly looked at Rupert. He didn't seem to notice.

Mandie, Celia, and Jonathan all caught their breath as they heard the housekeeper say, "The Baroness Geissler says she has also extended an invitation to the father of our young guest, Jonathan Guyer. He has not yet replied."

Senator Morton spoke up, "Why, that would be nice if Jonathan's father could visit while we're here."

"Jonathan!" Mandie gasped softly as she leaned across the table. "Do you think your father will really come?"

"I have no idea, but I would like to know how she knows my father," Jonathan replied.

"I can tell you that," Rupert spoke up. "My grandmother met your father at a ball in France not long ago, a charity ball, or something like that. He promised to visit my grandmother the next time he came to Germany. And since he is presently in Hamburg, she asked him to dinner."

"My father is in Hamburg? Right now?" Jonathan questioned. "How does she know that, when I don't even know it?"

"Aha!" Rupert replied with a knowing grin. "He is a widower, she is a widow. Maybe they were attracted to each other."

Jonathan gasped, and Mandie and Celia listened intently to the conversation.

"Besides," Rupert added. "Your father knows my mother and her American husband. They live near your father in New York. Did you not know that?"

"No, no, I didn't," Jonathan said, confused. "You see, I'm always gone to a boarding school somewhere. I'm not home much."

"I always had tutors stay here when I was your age," Rupert said. "Surely your father could afford tutors with all the money he has, instead of—"

Mandie quickly interrupted, "Of course Jonathan's father could afford tutors. But you see, we're Americans, and we don't do things the way you do them over here."

"You are right on that point," Rupert replied with disdain. "And we don't want to do things like the Americans do. Our way is much better."

Mandie felt her face burn with anger. She quickly asked, "Why do you not live with your mother in New York, Rupert?"

"There are several reasons why I do not live in the United States, none of which is your business," Rupert said haughtily.

Mandie noticed Frau Jahn's angry look at this last remark. She was no doubt aware of what they were talking about, or at least of Rupert's rude behavior. The baroness was speaking to the others in German, and when she paused for Frau Jahn to interpret, she turned to her grandson and smiled lovingly.

Rupert returned the smile and spoke to her in their language. Mandie was amazed at the way he could so suddenly change from being overly rude with her and her friends to being loving and attentive to the baroness.

When everyone had finished eating and they rose from the table, the baroness spoke again to Rupert and he replied cordially in German. Then his grandmother, with the help of Frau Jahn, invited the adults to the parlor, adding that Rupert would entertain the young people.

Mandie hurried around the long table to join Celia and Jonathan while Rupert took his time—pushing his chair up to the table, adjusting his jacket, slowly circling the table, and heading toward the door. By that time the adults had left the dining room.

As Rupert approached the young people he asked, "What would you like to do to be entertained?" He frowned as he waited for their answer.

"Could you show us through the castle?" Mandie asked.

"Yes, would you?" Celia added.

Jonathan remained silent, appraising the tall young man.

"Why, it would take days to go through this place," Rupert replied, sounding offended.

"Well then, show us whatever part you have time for," Mandie replied, determined that she would see as much of the old building as was possible.

"We will begin here, then," Rupert decided, indicating the dining room where they stood. "This is the smallest dining hall in our home. Now I will show you the largest." He led the way out the door, down a corridor, and then opened a set of huge double doors at the end. "And here is the largest." He motioned them inside.

The room was enormous. Several extra long, hand-carved tables were arranged in rows. Matching carved, red-upholstered chairs adorned each of them. Several elaborate chandeliers hung from the ceiling that was so high it seemed to reach the sky.

The three young people gasped in surprise as they took in the enormity of the room. Even their voices echoed as they spoke.

"So this is where your grandmother will have the dinner for the 'several hundred' guests she mentioned,"

Mandie remarked, walking around the tables, and running her hand along the soft, red plush upholstery.

"Yes, this is where we entertain, and believe me there has been some lavish entertainment in this room throughout the history of our castle—weddings, birthday parties, dinner parties; with special guests, including several presidents, kings, and queens from other countries," Rupert went on in a monotone as though he were reciting a speech. Then suddenly his speech quickened, and he added, "There have also been ghastly events here—murders, even cold-blooded murders." He held his breath and blew it out with a *whish*.

Celia shivered. But Mandie, knowing Rupert wanted to scare them, merely smiled and said, "Were you there when the murders took place?" She saw Jonathan grin at her.

Rupert seemed let down because he had not succeeded in frightening them. "Of course not. Those would have been duels—a long, long time ago when such things were permitted. People aren't murdered anymore over a simple disagreement."

"I hope not," Jonathan remarked. "Where is the dungeon? This place must have one, for all the prisoners who were captured in the feuds and wars so long ago, when your family were noblemen."

"Of course there is a dungeon. Follow me," Rupert told them as he quickly led them through various corridors, down two flights of stairs, and finally into an underground cavern where it was necessary to use candles for light.

The young people shivered as they gazed about the cool, dimly lit place.

"You can see some of the chains used to shackle the prisoners," Rupert explained as he bent to pick up the end of a heavy metal chain. Then he dropped it, and hurried toward another section. "And when they died, the prisoners were dumped into this pit and buried." He indicated a huge hole in the dirt floor.

The girls stayed close together as Jonathan spoke up, "All right. You've made your point, trying to upset the girls. Now let's go back upstairs where the air smells better."

"He hasn't upset me," Mandie protested. "We do study history in school, and we do learn about things like this. If he meant to scare us, he hasn't succeeded as far as I'm concerned."

Rupert tightened his lips as he glared at Mandie in the candlelight. Then he hurried toward the doorway and led the way out. They returned to the first floor of the castle where they had started, in silence. As they entered the dining hall corridor, Rupert stopped abruptly and announced, "I have no more time for you today. Do whatever you like." Then he quickly disappeared down the hallway and through a doorway at the end of it.

The three young people stood there a moment, stunned at Rupert's outrageous behavior.

"Let's find our way outside," Mandie suggested. "I want to see that jumping juniper tree that Olga told us about."

"Yes, let's do," Celia agreed.

"Anything outside would be better than the dreary, moldy interior of this place," Jonathan remarked.

The three had started down the hallway when Mandie suddenly stopped, "Oh, I better get Snowball. He'll need some fresh air, too. I believe the steps are this way." She started to her left down the corridor and Jonathan and Celia followed.

The hallways in this part of the castle were carpeted,

muting their footsteps as they hurried along, passing several closed doors. Then suddenly they heard laughter, and loud, merry talking in German from behind one of the doors. They stopped to listen.

"It's Rupert!" Mandie exclaimed under her breath. "It sounds like he's with a girl."

"Well, he is old enough to have a girlfriend," Jonathan teased. "Come on, let's go," he urged as he walked on.

"If you insist," Mandie replied with a smile as she and Celia followed him.

Chapter 5 / Mystery in the Woods

Jonathan waited for the girls in the hallway upstairs while Mandie and Celia went into their rooms to fetch Snowball.

Olga was hanging their clothes in the huge wardrobe.

"I hang all clothes in this one, since both you sleep in this one room," she told the girls. "All pressed, ready to use."

"Thank you, Olga," Mandie said, looking around the bedroom. "I came to take Snowball outside."

"Yes, thank you," Celia added.

"Shut in bathroom, cat is," the maid replied, picking up more clothes from chairs around the room and hanging them in the wardrobe.

Mandie found Snowball sitting on the bathroom floor, licking his paws and washing his face. There was an empty bowl before him. Apparently he had eaten everything the maid had brought.

"Come on, Snowball, we're going outside," Mandie

said, scooping him up and returning to the bedroom to get his red leash from the dresser. "I'd better fasten this on you, so you can't run away." He sat still in her lap as she hooked the leash to his collar, and jumped down as soon as she was finished.

"I think he's learned that when you put the leash on him, it means we're going out," Celia observed.

"I imagine so by now," Mandie replied. She glanced at her trunk as they walked by it. The lid was open, and she said to Olga, "I see you got my trunk opened."

"Yes, but, miss, look," Olga said, going over to the trunk. "The man had to break the lock."

"Oh, my!" Mandie exclaimed as she examined it. "How will I lock it again when we travel on?"

"We have trunks in the attic," the maid told her. "I will ask the baroness for another one for you."

"Ask the baroness for another *trunk*?" Mandie questioned her. "Can't the man repair the lock on mine?"

"He said not. It is impossible. Broken here and here," Olga said, pointing to the broken metal strips around the lock. "But do not worry. I get another trunk."

"From the attic?" Mandie said, her blue eyes twinkling. "Can we go with you to the attic?"

"If you like," Olga said, laying down the armful of clothes.

"Not right now, Olga. Jonathan is waiting for us to go outdoors," Mandie said. "Maybe later. When you have the time."

"Yes," Olga agreed, walking them to the door.

When Mandie and Celia joined Jonathan in the hallway, Mandie told him excitedly, "This castle has an attic! And we're going up there later with Olga to find another trunk for my clothes. The lock had to be broken to get mine open."

"That should be interesting," Jonathan replied as they walked down the hallway toward the stairs.

"Yes, if the attic is as old as the rest of this castle, imagine what could be up there!" Mandie said enthusiastically, leading Snowball along by his leash.

"Mandie, wouldn't anything that old be rotten or rusted by now?" Celia asked as they turned down the steps.

"Maybe," Mandie agreed. "But there should be lots of old things in good condition too, if it's at all like other attics I've been in."

Jonathan stopped at the bottom of the steps and pointed to the left. "I believe the outside door is this way."

They opened the door and stepped outside. The sun was shining, but it didn't seem as bright as the sun back home. The sky looked gray as Mandie viewed it through the foliage of the trees.

"This is the door we came in from the carriage," Mandie remarked as they looked around. "Let's go to the other side of the house where the drawbridge is. Olga said the juniper tree is near it."

The three walked through the irregular flower gardens toward the end of the castle. The grounds of other mansions they had visited had neat, planned gardens. This estate seemed to have a more casual, natural look, with trees and shrubbery scattered about here and there, and odd-shaped beds of blooming greenery in disarray. But Mandie noticed everything was freshly cut and clean.

"There!" Mandie said as they rounded the corner. She pointed to a huge juniper tree. "That must be the one."

They stopped to look.

"Yes, it does seem to be the largest tree here," Jonathan agreed.

"But it's just a plain old juniper tree. How could it

possibly jump up and down?" Celia commented.

"That's what we're going to find out," Mandie replied, securing Snowball's leash as he tried to get away.

"And how do you propose doing that?" Jonathan asked.

"Well," Mandie said thoughtfully, gazing at the tree. "We could just stand here and watch it until it moves."

"Couldn't we at least sit down?" Celia asked.

"Yes, let's get comfortable. If we're going to wait for that tree to jump up and down, it could be an awfully long time," Jonathan said. He looked around and spotted a low wall nearby. "Why don't we sit over there?"

"Shall we see the rest of the yard first?" Mandie asked, turning the next corner of the castle. "Look! There's the moat and drawbridge. Just like the pictures in our history book."

Jonathan and Celia followed her. The three stopped at the drawbridge, which was open, and looked inside.

"My goodness! It looks like the carriage is in there!" Mandie exclaimed.

"Yes it is," Jonathan said. "That was the original purpose of the drawbridge, to allow travelers to enter the walls of the castle. When everyone was safely inside, the drawbridge was pulled up to conceal the carriage from the enemy or passersby."

"And there are no windows large enough to enter on the ground floor, just those slits in the walls," Mandie said.

"What a good idea," Celia said.

After walking completely around the castle, looking at all the surroundings, the three arrived back at the huge juniper tree and sat down on the low wall to watch and wait.

"Well, if that tree decides to move, we'll be sure to see

it from here," Jonathan remarked.

"I don't really think it will move," Mandie admitted, tying Snowball's leash to a nearby bush.

"Then what are we waiting for?" Celia asked.

"There has to be some kind of mystery about it," Mandie replied. "A huge tree like that couldn't possibly jump up and down. Evidently someone is just making up tales about it. If we wait long enough, maybe we'll find out something."

They watched and waited for a long time and nothing happened. Their conversation turned to other things.

"What are you going to wear to dinner tomorrow night, Mandie?" Celia asked.

"I don't know," Mandie replied. "Since Grandmother asked us to leave many of our things in the hotel in London in order not to be bogged down with luggage, I don't remember exactly what I brought. I'll have to see."

"I doubt that my father will come to that dinner," Jonathan remarked as he drew circles in the dirt with a stick.

"I hope he doesn't," Mandie confided. "Because he could decide to take you back home, and I'd like you to travel on with us. Besides, we haven't even met your aunt and uncle in Paris yet."

"If they ever return home, I might be able to talk my father into letting me visit with them awhile," Jonathan said, straightening up and brushing the sand from his hands.

"And then we'd finally get to meet them," Celia added. "They sure do travel a lot. They seem to be always off to somewhere else as soon as they return to Paris."

"Well, you know people who work for newspapers. They always travel a lot," Jonathan explained.

"Just like Uncle Ned," Mandie said. "He's always

going somewhere. I hope he gets here in time for the dinner tomorrow night."

"Mandie, I don't think this tree is ever going to move," Jonathan said, standing up. "How about walking around beyond the grounds a bit? We can always come back and check on the tree."

"Well, all right," Mandie agreed, untying Snowball's leash from the bush. "Which way do you want to go? It looks like the place is completely surrounded by forest."

Celia looked around and then pointed. "I see a pathway over there. Why don't we see where it leads?"

The others agreed and the three started down the lane that led away into the trees on the side of the castle. The ground was firm, evidently well-traveled, Mandie decided as they went along. Here and there she noticed dried hoof-prints in the dirt. The trees on either side were so thick it was impossible to see very far through them.

Suddenly they came into a clearing with a small hut in the center of it. Even though it looked old, there were lace curtains in the windows, and a few flowers bloomed against the wall of the tiny house.

The three young people stood there staring at the cottage, Snowball straining at his leash.

"What do you suggest we do?" Jonathan asked.

"Let's knock on the door and see if anyone's home," Mandie answered.

"There's no telling who could be living there, Mandie," Celia objected. "They might not like strangers coming up to their door uninvited."

"I don't think they'd mind. It's probably someone who works for the castle. We're still on the estate property, as far as I know," Mandie replied.

As they discussed whether they would knock, the door to the hut suddenly opened, and who should step outside, but Rupert! The three young people gasped in surprise.

Rupert paused when he saw them, then closed the door quickly behind him, and strode forward on the pathway without speaking a word. He held his head high and frowned angrily, ignoring them completely.

For once, none of the three spoke. Mandie couldn't think of a thing to say. After the way Rupert had behaved toward them earlier, she had decided to leave him alone. But they all turned to watch until he was out of sight down the pathway toward the castle.

"Well!" Mandie said, blowing out her breath. "I wonder who lives here, and what Rupert was doing inside the house?"

"It must belong to the castle," Jonathan remarked, "and whoever lives in it must work for Rupert's family. He was no doubt here on castle business, don't you think?"

"Maybe," Mandie said as they stood still, again staring at the small house. Then she saw the curtain move, and was sure a young woman inside was watching them. "Don't look now, but I just saw a woman behind those curtains in the right-hand window."

Jonathan and Celia nonchalantly rolled their eyes toward the right-hand window without moving.

"I see her, too," Celia agreed.

"And so do I," Jonathan said. "She's probably a maid at the castle."

"Why do you think Rupert was visiting her?" Mandie asked. She watched the window. "The woman looks vaguely familiar. She has long black hair, and looks a few years older than I am."

"You're right, Mandie," Celia said.

"We can't just stand here all day staring at the hut," Jonathan reminded them. "Are we going on down the pathway around this clearing, or are we going back to the castle?"

"Let's walk on for a while," Mandie said, looking at Celia.

"All right, let's go on," Celia agreed.

The pathway made a wide arc past the house and then descended a steep hillside. As the three paused to look ahead, they could see the distant mountains as well as the green meadows below. The trees had thinned out here, and the grass made a luxurious carpet under their feet until it reached the edge of the downgrade. Then rocks formed the pathway with low bushes and wild flowers along the sides.

"Oh, it's beautiful!" Mandie said, looking beyond where they stood.

"It's also a pretty rough and steep path," Jonathan reminded her as he gazed at the trail leading down the embankment.

"I see another path over this way," Celia said, pointing to her left.

Mandie looked in that direction and said, "You're right. And it goes right into the woods."

"Let's try it," Jonathan said. "It looks easier."

They began walking in that direction. The pathway looked a lot like the first one, but was almost swallowed up by the huge trees that also shut out most of the sunlight.

After a while they came to a fork in the pathway. It split to the left and right. They stopped to choose their way.

"Right or left?" Mandie asked.

"The paths look the same," Jonathan remarked.

"Let's go to the left," Celia decided.

"Why?" Mandie asked, looking to the left.

"I think I see some beautiful flowers up ahead on the path," Celia said as she walked on.

As they neared the bright colors, Mandie looked about for birds or animals. There didn't seem to be anything living in the forest.

When they finally got close enough to see the area beyond the flowers, they discovered another cottage situated by the trail. The flowers seemed to belong to the occupant. The house was similar to the one they had just seen. Lace curtains adorned the windows, and the shingles looked old.

As Mandie stood there wishing they could pick the flowers, she noticed a faint spiral of smoke coming from the chimney.

"Someone must be home. I see smoke from a fire," she told her friends.

"It looks like the estate owns several cottages in the woods for the workers to live in," Jonathan remarked.

Just then, an elderly woman emerged from the front door. She had a homemade broom, and was intent on sweeping the stoop. At first she didn't seem to notice the young people as they watched and waited. But when she descended the short flight of steps, sweeping them off as she went, she finally looked up and saw them. She backed up the steps, staring at the strangers.

"Hello," Mandie called to her as she walked forward. "We are visiting at the castle."

The woman backed into the doorway and held the door open, as if ready to dart inside. Her eyes didn't waver from them.

Mandie and the others moved closer, cautiously.

"Do you understand English?" Mandie asked.

The woman still didn't utter a word, but stood there transfixed.

"Sprechen Sie Englisch?" Jonathan asked her.

"Nein, nein, nein!" the woman quickly replied.

"What did you say to her? She looks scared," Mandie said.

"I only asked her if she speaks English and she said 'no,'" he explained.

"Well then, say something to her in German," Mandie said.

"I don't know much," Jonathan admitted. Then he turned back to the old woman and said, "Guten Tag."

The woman immediately replied in a rush of German, and Jonathan couldn't understand a word she was saying. "Sorry, I don't know what that's all about. Maybe we'd better go," Jonathan said.

Mandie suddenly remembered the words Frau Jahn had taught her that morning to thank the baroness. "Vielen Dank," she called to the woman.

"But what are you thanking her for, Mandie?" Celia asked, also remembering what the German words meant.

The woman smiled, waved to them, and went inside the cottage, closing the door behind her.

"Those are the only words I know," Mandie said. "I wish I knew more, so I could talk to the people we meet."

"You can always learn," Jonathan said with his mischievous smile.

"That would take too long. I want to be able to speak to them right now, during our trip here to Europe," Mandie replied.

"I think you ought to learn some languages when you go back to school, so you'll be able to talk to people the next time you travel over here," Jonathan said. "French is probably a good one to learn, and of course German, and some Italian."

"Whew! That sounds like a lot of work," Mandie said

as she held tightly to Snowball's leash. "You don't know that much yourself, Jonathan."

"No, but I am learning at school," he said. "After you get to know one foreign language, it's not all that hard to learn another."

"I am definitely going to take some languages this next school year," Celia said.

"I think we ought to go back now and watch the juniper tree before it's time for another meal or something," Mandie said.

They turned around and started back. A short way down the pathway, Mandie suddenly stopped and held her hands up to the others.

"I hear something," she said softly, listening.

Jonathan and Celia waited silently.

"It's a horse," Mandie decided.

The others also heard it. It was a clip-clopping sound, and it was coming toward them.

"Let's wait behind those trees over there and see who it is," Mandie told the others as they all ran for cover.

"The horse does not have a rider, Mandie," Celia spoke up.

"How do you know?" Jonathan asked in a whisper.

"Because the gait is not right. Listen," Celia explained.

"I think you're right," Mandie said softly as they all watched the pathway. "It sure is moving slowly."

They waited impatiently, and then as the horse began to appear through the trees, Mandie suddenly put her hands to her mouth and gave a shrill bird-like call. "It's Uncle Ned!" she cried. "I see him!" She pointed excitedly through the thick trees and ran out onto the pathway. Celia and Jonathan followed.

In seconds an answering call was returned. Mandie stood in the middle of the trail, practically jumping up and down as she waited for her old Indian friend to appear on the pathway.

In a few moments Uncle Ned came walking slowly toward them, leading his horse. A big grin covered his face as he saw the young people.

Mandie ran to grab his hand and squeeze it. "Uncle Ned, I'm so glad you've finally gotten here. We had a wreck, got lost, and had quite a time getting to the castle. And, there is a huge juniper tree on the property that jumps up and down!"

"Papoose!" the old man said, trying to calm her. "A wreck? Anyone hurt?" He looked worried.

"No, we didn't get hurt, but we got lost," Mandie explained. "And if we'd had you with us we wouldn't have gotten lost."

Uncle Ned smiled down at her as he put an arm around her slim shoulders.

"You find tree that jumps up and down?" he asked.

"The maid, Olga is her name, says the tree is known to do it, and we've been watching, but it hasn't moved yet," Mandie spoke rapidly. "We were on the way back to look at it now."

"We all go see," Uncle Ned said as they resumed walking along the pathway.

"Why are you walking, Uncle Ned?" Celia asked.

"Horse throw a shoe," he explained.

"I'm sure they have stables here somewhere," Jonathan offered. "And someone who can put a new shoe on."

"Yes, they must have, because they have horses, too," Celia reminded them. "And they're so wealthy, they probably have their own shop."

Mandie looked up at the tall Indian and said, "I hope

you haven't had to walk a long way. But we're almost to the castle now."

When they came within view of the huge structure, they all stopped for Uncle Ned to get a good look. Then Mandie ran forward to point out the tall juniper tree.

"This is it, Uncle Ned, right here," she said as she stood beneath it. "And I can't see that it has moved any."

"No way tree can jump up and down," Uncle Ned said, looking up at it.

"But the maid said it has been known to several times," Mandie repeated.

Uncle Ned smiled at Mandie, his black eyes twinkling. "Maid tell Papoose tale. Make exciting story."

Mandie looked crestfallen as she realized that Olga might have indeed been making up the story. After all, Rupert had denied knowing anything about the tree jumping up and down.

She tilted her head back as she looked up at Uncle Ned and said solemnly, "Maybe," and then with a little smile, she added, "And maybe not. Anyway we are going to find out."

Mandie decided then and there that she would put an end to Olga's story, one way or the other.

Chapter 6 / Watching the Juniper Tree

As Mandie led the way to the back of the castle in search of a blacksmith or stable boy to take Uncle Ned's horse, they met a small, dark young man who stopped to speak to them.

"If you wish, sir, I will take the horse for you," he offered. "My name is Ludwig. I am on the way to the stables to inspect the baroness's racehorses. I am the jockey."

Uncle Ned looked down at the smiling young man and handed over the reins to him. "Many thanks. Horse need shoe," he said.

"*Ja*, I noticed the horse is not walking right," Ludwig replied as he took the reins and bent to look at the animal's foot. "I will attend to it."

"You have racehorses here?" Celia asked excitedly. "We raise racehorses back home in Virginia."

Ludwig smiled at Celia and said, "Yes, we have had many winners. Please allow me to show you our horses."

"Oh, I'd love to see them," Celia replied, and turning

to her friends, she asked, "Shall we?"

"Of course, Celia, but maybe later," Mandie replied. "I think we ought to go on inside with Uncle Ned. My grandmother may be wondering where we are." And then with a big smile, she added, "I want to see them, too."

"All right," Celia agreed. "We have been out an awfully long time. Ludwig, we'll let you know when we can come look."

A uniformed servant came out into the yard, and walked directly to the horse.

"I will take your luggage, sir," he told Uncle Ned as he began unhooking the bags from the animal's back.

Uncle Ned helped him and said, "Thank you. I not know where to take them."

"I know exactly where, sir. We have your rooms all ready for you. The baroness informed us of your tentative arrival," the servant said. "Please follow me," he said, picking up the bags.

Uncle Ned was wearing his deerskin jacket, and he took his bow and arrows from the horse and slung them over his shoulder. The servant and Ludwig both watched curiously.

"Uncle Ned is a Cherokee Indian," Mandie explained as she saw the two men's puzzled expressions. "I am also one-fourth Cherokee. My grandmother was full-blooded."

"Ja, Ja," Ludwig said. "I will wait to hear more when you come to see the racehorses." He led the horse away down the path.

The servant hurried toward the back door of the castle, and everyone scrambled to catch up with him, all except Uncle Ned, that is. He never seemed to hurry, because his long legs could make such long strides.

Entering the house through the back way, they found

themselves in an old kitchen. The walls were made of stone. At one side was a huge open fireplace. And on the other side there stood what seemed to be a well. Mandie rushed over to look.

"You have a well inside the kitchen?" she asked. The other young people crowded around to see.

"We do not use this kitchen anymore, since about one hundred years ago, in fact, but that is a well. Back then, the family had to have all such necessities inside the castle in case of a siege by the enemy, when it would be impossible to go outside," he explained. Then turning to lead the way, he added, "Now, please come this way."

They followed the man through a maze of corridors, up one flight of stairs, and down another. Finally they arrived in the hallway where they were shown Uncle Ned's suite. It was located near their own.

"This is your suite, sir," the servant told Uncle Ned as he pushed open a heavy, ornate door.

Uncle Ned followed him inside, while the young people peered in behind him at the heavy antique furnishings, and elaborate decor of the sitting room. Then the servant threw open a second door, revealing an enormous bedroom.

Snowball, who had been content in Mandie's arms until now, wriggled to get down. Mandie put him up on her shoulder.

"Why don't we leave Uncle Ned to freshen up after his long journey?" Jonathan suggested.

"Of course," Mandie agreed.

"Yes, he must be awfully tired," Celia added.

Uncle Ned smiled and said, "Not much tired, but dirty. I wash up and then find Papoose and friends."

Mandie led the way out into the hall and said, "I see Olga down there. She can tell us how to get to the parlor."

"I will unpack your things, and show you where to find the others when you are ready," Mandie heard the servant say to Uncle Ned.

Jonathan whistled for Olga, and the maid turned and came toward them, laughing.

"You are American all right," she said with a smile.

Mandie asked, "Could you please show us where the adults are? They are probably in the parlor."

"Yes, miss," Olga said, turning to walk back down the hallway. "This way."

After following Olga through the corridors and down stairs, they arrived at the entrance to an enormous drawing room. It was decorated in satin, silk, and velvet, in various shades of lavender and purple. It was filled to the point of being crowded with lavish-looking antiques.

Mrs. Taft, Senator Morton, and Baroness Geissler were all seated. Frau Jahn stood to the side, still acting as interpreter for the baroness.

"Oh, dear, where have y'all been?" Mrs. Taft asked as they entered the room. "You've missed tea because we couldn't find y'all."

The baroness motioned for them to sit down.

"We've been for a walk, Grandmother, and Uncle Ned just arrived," Mandie said, explaining how they had met up with him in the woods. "He's in his room now."

"Well, I'm glad he finally got here. I was worried that he was lost or something, too," Mrs. Taft said.

"Is he coming down?" Senator Morton asked.

"As soon as he gets cleaned up," Mandie replied, holding on to Snowball as he struggled to get down.

"That's good, because we are discussing the dinner party for tomorrow night, and the baroness was hoping he'd get here in time for that," Mrs. Taft said.

Baroness Geissler spoke rapidly in German and Frau

Jahn told them, "We have received a reply from Mr. Guyer and he will not be able to come. He said he is leaving Germany today to go to France where he will visit relatives with whom his son wished to stay."

Jonathan asked, "Did he say I could go visit with my aunt and uncle in Paris?"

Frau Jahn and the baroness exchanged a few words in German and then the housekeeper said, "He did not state any decision about your visiting, only that he will visit the people you refer to."

Mandie looked at Jonathan as he sighed deeply. She knew that he would like to get his future settled, whether it meant going to live with his aunt and uncle in Paris, or going home to New York with his father.

Uncle Ned joined them then, as the servant showed him into the room. Mandie noticed that the baroness looked agitated as she was introduced to him through the housekeeper. There followed a barrage of questions and answers as the woman inquired about the Cherokees. The housekeeper had trouble interpreting Uncle Ned's broken English, and several times Mandie had to explain to her what the old Indian was saying.

By the time all this was accomplished, the young people were told to go upstairs and get ready for the evening meal.

Mandie, Celia, and Jonathan discussed various things as they tried to find their way back to their rooms. They had declined help from the maid, but did accept her instructions on how to get through the enormous castle.

"I wonder where Rupert is," Mandie remarked as she let Snowball run along on his leash.

"Probably avoiding us," Jonathan said.

"I sure don't think he likes us," Celia agreed.

As they talked, a door along the corridor opened and

closed, and Rupert stood there looking at them. They slowed their steps, but didn't stop, and no one spoke. They were relieved when they saw him go off in the opposite direction.

When they had gotten to the corner of the hallway, they glanced back and saw someone coming out of another door.

Mandie quickly whispered to her friends, "That's the woman who was inside that cottage in the woods."

"She must be a maid here. She's wearing a uniform," Jonathan said under his breath as the young woman rapidly approached them.

"Right," Celia whispered.

The woman passed them in the hallway, but didn't even look at them. They all stared at her. She had long black hair, and was quite pretty. The uniform she was wearing was similar to the one Olga wore.

"Well!" Mandie exclaimed.

"She and Rupert must be sweet on each other," Jonathan remarked as they reached the doors to their rooms.

"Either that or they're in cahoots about something or other," Mandie said.

"We meet up with a lot of interesting people, don't we?" Celia added.

"See you girls back downstairs," Jonathan said, entering his suite and closing the door.

Inside their rooms, the girls flipped through their clothes hanging in the wardrobe.

"I suppose I'll have to save this blue silk for tomorrow night. It's too fancy for an ordinary dinner, anyway," Mandie decided as she pushed it aside and selected a pink dress. "I'll wear this tonight."

"I think I'll wear my white dress with the pink and blue embroidered flowers tomorrow night," Celia said. "For tonight, this tan dress will do."

The girls didn't take long to change clothes and redo their hair.

"You know, Celia, I think we ought to go back and watch that juniper tree after dark tonight. Olga said it jumped up and down last night. Maybe it only does it at night," Mandie said as they hurried down the hallway.

She had left Snowball in their suite, where she knew Olga would feed him.

"After dark, Mandie? Do you think that's safe?" Celia asked.

"Sure. There are plenty of people working around here, all day and all night. Senator Morton said so," Mandie assured her.

"But this is a strange place to us," her friend objected.

"Oh, Celia, we'll ask Jonathan to go with us. He'll want to go anyway," Mandie said.

"What about Uncle Ned? Couldn't we ask him to go too? He's big and strong, and I'd feel safer with him," Celia suggested.

"No, Celia, we can't ask him. We won't even go out there until after everyone is in bed," Mandie said. "Besides, he doesn't believe the tree really moves. Remember what he said about Olga telling tales?"

Jonathan came rushing up behind them just then.

"You girls sure did get ready fast," he said. "I thought I'd beat you downstairs."

Mandie told him about their plans to watch the tree after everyone had retired for the night. He sounded interested.

"Sure I'll go," he said. "In fact, you girls had better not go without me." He smiled mischievously.

Mandie heard someone behind them, and glanced back in time to see Rupert right at their heels. Evidently he had been following quietly, so as not to be detected.

Mandie boldly turned around and asked, "Are you on the way downstairs to dinner, Rupert?"

"Of course I am. Where do you think I would be going?" he asked sullenly as he brushed past them and hurried ahead.

When they arrived at the drawing room, everyone was ready to go in to dinner.

Mandie found herself seated next to Rupert, and was frustrated because she couldn't talk to her friends without him hearing everything.

The baroness spoke rapidly in German to her grandson and Rupert replied. Frau Jahn stood by listening and frowning. Mandie also noticed her shake her head in silence, and her lips tighten in apparent anger. But the baroness seemed to be in a good mood and happy with everyone.

Mrs. Taft and Senator Morton spoke to each other, and Mandie saw them look at the baroness and then at Rupert. Uncle Ned was seated on the other side of Rupert.

The baroness suddenly stood up and made a remark to the housekeeper. Frau Jahn said, smiling, "The baroness wishes to inform you that Fraulein Elsa Wagner will be arriving tonight to stay a few days. She is the fiancee of the baroness's grandson, here present."

Everyone turned and smiled at the baroness.

He's engaged to be married! Mandie thought, swiftly remembering the flirtatious way Rupert conducted himself around other girls. *Well, it is a good idea for that Elsa Wagner to come and check up on him!*

As soon as the meal was over, everyone returned to the drawing room. The adults carried on a conversation with the assistance of Frau Jahn. The young people sat together almost in silence, because Rupert chose a seat near them.

When Mandie suggested they walk outside for some fresh air, he suddenly decided to accompany them.

Once outside, Rupert quickly disappeared into the woods without any explanation.

As they watched him go, Mandie suggested, "We might as well go look at that tree while we're out here."

The tree did not appear to have moved.

"I don't believe that tree has ever moved. How could it?" Jonathan declared.

"Well, we'll just come back out here later and watch for a while," Mandie said. "I'd like to find out where the rumor started anyway. Let's go find Olga and talk to her."

They went back inside the castle, but when they finally located Olga, she wouldn't say anything more about the tree, except that it had been seen to jump up and down.

"And you didn't see it yourself?" Mandie asked in an upstairs hallway.

"No, miss, never, but other people have," the maid insisted.

"What other people?" Mandie asked. "Tell us who these other people are."

"Well, I shouldn't, but I will tell you. One person who saw it was the new maid, the French one named Yvette," Olga explained.

"With the long black hair?" Jonathan asked.

"And does Yvette live in a cottage in the woods?" Mandie asked before Olga could answer Jonathan.

"A cottage in the woods?" Olga suddenly withdrew, frowning. "No, miss, she has a room upstairs."

Olga left them abruptly. The three young people looked at each other in puzzlement.

"Maybe the woman doesn't live in the cottage. Maybe she was just out there for some reason," Celia suggested.

"The one we saw may not be the girl named Yvette," Jonathan said.

"I just feel that it is the same girl," Mandie said. "Let's see if we can find her. We don't have to let her know that Olga told us she was the one who had seen the tree jump."

So they began a search through the castle for the maid named Yvette.

Chapter 7 / The Secret in the Well

The three young people looked for Yvette, but the inside of the castle was growing dark as night came. In some places the corridors were so dimly lit that it was hard for them to see their way around. Once in a while they saw a servant hurrying about on chores.

Then suddenly they came upon double doors in a hallway, and as Jonathan pushed them open they found themselves in complete blackness.

"Oh, let's go back!" Celia exclaimed as she stopped short.

Mandie stood still, trying to see ahead. "We sure need some kind of light," she said.

"I don't think Yvette would be in this part of the castle anyway, because it seems to be all dark from here on," Jonathan told the girls.

"We'll just have to come back here in the daytime when there's enough light to see," Mandie decided as she turned to go back.

"How are we going to find it again?" Celia asked as the three started down the corridor the way they had come.

"I have lost all sense of direction," Jonathan said.

"We could stop and look out a window from one of the rooms in this hallway and see what's outside. Then when we do come back up here, we would have some idea as to what part of the castle we're in," Mandie reasoned.

As she spoke, Mandie led the way into a room nearby and the three hurried over to a window, guided by the faint light from the hallway. They pulled back the curtain. It appeared they were above the front doorway.

"Look at all the lights outside!" Mandie exclaimed. "I don't remember seeing that many last night when Senator Morton and I got here."

"But there is someone special coming tonight, remember, Mandie? Rupert's fiancee," Celia reminded her.

"I wonder what time she is expected?" Jonathan remarked as they looked down into the yard.

"No one spoke of a time," Mandie replied. "I listened at the table. Frau Jahn just said the baroness told her Elsa Wagner would be here tonight."

"Do you suppose she is already here?" Celia asked.

"She could have arrived while we've been going through the castle," Jonathan said. "I think we ought to find our way back downstairs."

"Yes. Let's go find out," Mandie decided.

The three hadn't gone very far down the corridor when they spied Olga rushing down a cross hall.

"Olga!" Mandie called to her as she hurried to catch up with the maid.

Olga stopped and looked in their direction. "Yes, miss?" she said.

"Do you know if Rupert's fiancee has arrived yet?" Mandie asked as the three reached the cross hall.

"No, miss, but she is due anytime now. So I must hurry," Olga replied as she quickly disappeared down another intersecting corridor.

"Why don't we go camp out somewhere near the front door and watch for her?" Mandie suggested.

"Yes, I'd like to see what she looks like," Celia agreed.

"It might be interesting to see what kind of girl would marry that Rupert," Jonathan said with a smile.

They rushed down one corridor after another until they finally found themselves in the section where their rooms were located.

"Now we know where we are," Mandie remarked. "The stairs are in that direction." She pointed ahead.

"Right," Jonathan agreed.

After getting down to the first floor they finally located the front door, or the door through which they had come when they arrived. To Mandie it seemed to be in the back of the castle, but then this wasn't an ordinary house.

"We could sit on that bench over there and watch for a while," Mandie said, leading the way to a long bench by a table at one side of the huge doorway.

They didn't have long to wait before they heard a carriage pulling up outside. Then suddenly servants seemed to come from everywhere as they all rushed toward the door. The tall, slender butler hurried to throw open the front door, Frau Jahn standing by his side.

No one seemed to notice the young people, and now they stood up and moved a little closer to the door. Two different female voices could be heard outside.

"Hurry now, Elsa," a woman was saying in English.

"Oh, Aunt Wilhelmina, I am so tired and crumpled," a younger female voice replied.

The butler moved forward as the two women approached the doorway. "Guten Abend, Gnadige Frau Schiller, Fraulein Wagner," he greeted them. "We await your presence."

"Good evening," the older woman replied as she stepped through the doorway, followed by the younger woman.

Frau Jahn gave a courteous nod and said, "Gnadige Frau Schiller, Fraulein Wagner, I will show you to your suite where you may refresh yourselves, and then the Baroness Geissler will be waiting for you in the drawing room."

"Ja, danke," the older woman replied.

The three young people shrank back into the shadows of the hallway as the housekeeper led the two women down the hallway. Both of the new guests were enveloped in full dark cloaks, and it was impossible to see their faces from where Mandie and her friends stood watching.

The servants hurriedly followed the ladies with their many pieces of luggage from the carriage. And suddenly the hallway was empty except for the three young people.

"Well, what were they saying, Jonathan? Could you understand those German words?" Mandie asked.

"Simple. The butler merely greeted them with 'Good evening, Madam Schiller, Miss Wagner.' Then the older woman said, 'Yes, thank you.' That was all," the boy explained.

"The woman must be the girl's aunt, since she called her Aunt Wilhelmina. I wonder why her mother didn't come with her," Celia remarked.

"Maybe her mother is deceased—or something," Mandie said, and then quickly added, "We should have watched to see where their rooms are. Let's go!"

She led the way down the corridor and up the stairs,

her friends close behind. At the top they paused to look around and listen. There was no one in sight, and not a sound to be heard.

"Maybe they went in the opposite direction," Jonathan suggested as they stood there. "Our rooms are that way." He pointed to the left. "And they could have gone that way." He pointed right.

"Right," Mandie agreed as she quickly led them in the opposite direction.

Although they went up and down corridors and listened at doorways, they couldn't locate the new guests.

"If we go back to the top of the stairs and wait, they will probably come back down that way to meet the baroness in the drawing room," Mandie told her friends.

"Mandie, there are several sets of stairs in this castle. You know that," Jonathan reminded.

"I know, but the stairs we use seem to be the ones everyone else goes up and down," Mandie replied.

"Mandie, your grandmother is probably wondering where we are, and when the new guests go to the drawing room we should be there to be introduced," Celia told her.

"Oh, yes, you're right," Mandie agreed with a sigh. "We'd better go back to the drawing room."

The young people walked three abreast down the hallway toward the stairs. As Mandie led them through double dividing doors to a connecting corridor, a young girl was coming from the other hallway and they collided.

"*Pardon!*" the girl exclaimed in French as she glanced at Mandie.

"Please excuse me," Mandie replied. "I believe it was my fault." She looked at the young lady, dressed in a dark, ruffled dress. Her thick dark hair was piled high on her head, and her dark eyes looked curiously at Mandie and her friends.

"So be it," the girl replied, and turned to go on.

"My name is Amanda Shaw, Mandie for short, and these are my friends, Celia Hamilton and Jonathan Guyer," Mandie quickly said.

The other girl didn't even turn to look at her again, but hurried on down the corridor.

Mandie murmured to her friends, "Rupert's fiancee certainly doesn't have any manners."

"We'd better go on down to the drawing room, Mandie," Jonathan said.

"Yes, and then she'll have to stand still long enough to be introduced to us," Mandie agreed.

The night had grown chilly and a fire was roaring in the huge fireplace in the drawing room. Evidently Elsa's aunt had gone on down ahead of the girl, because she was already seated, and Baroness Geissler was introducing Elsa Wagner to Mrs. Taft and Senator Morton, with Frau Jahn's help. Elsa was standing before them as the young people paused in the doorway.

Mrs. Taft spoke to the girl, "I am pleased to meet you, dear."

Elsa merely nodded her head and took a seat nearby as Senator Morton said, "It is indeed a pleasure to meet you, Miss Wagner."

The young people walked on into the room and Mrs. Taft saw them.

"Oh, Amanda, please come over here," Mrs. Taft said to her granddaughter.

"You must meet Rupert's fiancee." She beckoned to the young people. "And you, too, Celia, and Jonathan."

When Mandie and her friends approached Mrs. Taft, Mandie glanced at Elsa. The girl was not even looking at them.

"Miss Wagner, this is my granddaughter, Amanda

Shaw, and her friends, Celia Hamilton, and Jonathan Guyer," Mrs. Taft said, looking at the young girl.

Elsa Wagner turned to glance at the three and merely nodded her head, then immediately spoke rapidly in German to Baroness Geissler. Whatever she said, the older woman laughed and then replied something else they could not understand.

Mrs. Taft looked slightly upset as she caught Senator Morton's look and raised her eyebrows. Elsa's aunt sat silently watching.

Mandie looked at her friends and frowned. Celia quickly went to sit on a settee near the senator, and Mandie and Jonathan followed. The three sat there gazing at Elsa, not understanding a word she was saying to the baroness.

Frau Jahn evidently had noticed the exchange among the American guests. She smiled at Mrs. Taft and said softly, as Elsa continued to talk to the baroness, "She is tired. Long journey she has had today."

"Yes," Mrs. Taft muttered with a strained smile at the housekeeper.

Suddenly the baroness turned to Frau Jahn and spoke to her. Frau Jahn translated for Mrs. Taft. "The baroness asks that you please forgive her necessary conversation with Fraulein Wagner. She will dispense with it shortly."

"Thank you," Mrs. Taft said.

The aunt spoke then, "They are discussing the arrangements for the dinner party tomorrow night." Then turning to the young people across the room, she added, "I am Frau Schiller, Fraulein Wagner's aunt. It is nice to meet you young Americans."

"Thank you, ma'am," the three young people chimed.

"I am sorry, Frau Schiller. Please forgive my manners. I simply forgot to introduce them to you," Mrs. Taft said, somewhat hastily.

"Of course, madam. You have beautiful young people in your care," Frau Schiller replied.

"Thank you," Mrs. Taft said. "It is a job, keeping up with them."

"You're right on that score," Senator Morton said, smiling at the two ladies.

Mandie suddenly realized her old Cherokee friend was not present.

"Grandmother, where is Uncle Ned?" she asked.

"He has gone for a walk. He'll be back soon," Mrs. Taft told her. "And you might tell me where your kitten is, dear."

"Oh, he's in our suite," Mandie explained. "Olga feeds him in our bathroom, so I just leave him there."

Mandie glanced at Elsa's aunt while the woman was not looking at them. The woman didn't seem to be much older than Elsa, but she had a more mature figure. Her hair and eyes were also dark, and she was wearing a simple black dress and no jewelry.

Mrs. Taft was talking to Frau Schiller. "Will Miss Wagner's mother also be coming for the dinner tomorrow night?" she asked the German woman.

"Nein, no, madam," Frau Schiller replied with a sad expression on her face. "Elsa's mother passed to the beyond last year and Elsa was left alone, her father having been deceased for many years. Since a young lady must have proper supervision I moved into the house with her. When she marries Rupert next year, they will live there and I shall return to my own estate."

"I am sorry about her family," Mrs. Taft said. "So they will not be wed until next year?"

"That is correct. You see, we are just now coming out of our period of mourning. Once that is past we have many things to accomplish before the wedding," Frau Schiller explained.

Mrs. Taft looked around and asked, "I haven't seen Rupert. Was he not here to greet his bride-to-be?"

"The Baroness Geissler explained that he is away on a short journey of business and will return soon," Frau Schiller said.

Mandie and her friends looked at each other. Where had Rupert gone?

He had followed them outside after dinner and had vanished into the woods. *Some business in the woods*, Mandie thought. He must not be really interested in Elsa, considering the way he was acting.

Baroness Geissler finished her conversation with Elsa and spoke to Mrs. Taft and the senator through Frau Jahn's interpretation. Elsa seemed to be in deep thought and wasn't really paying any attention to anyone.

"The baroness says we will have guests arriving to-morrow from several different countries. Some of them are American and you may be acquainted with them," Frau Jahn said.

"Oh, please tell me the names," Mrs. Taft said to her.

Mandie and her friends began their own conversation, quietly enough that Elsa could not hear what they were saying.

"I wish it would hurry up and be time for everyone to go to bed, so we can go outside and watch the juniper tree," Mandie whispered.

"Yes, well, it—" Jonathan began, and then the cuckoo clock on the mantelpiece interrupted with its shrill call to announce the hour of ten o'clock. Everyone looked at it.

Mrs. Taft gasped and said, "Oh, dear, I didn't realize

it was so late." She turned to the young people. "I think you should all get to bed now. We'll rise early in the morning to prepare for a busy day."

Mandie and her friends rose to say good night. At that moment Uncle Ned came into the room. He was still wearing his leather jacket and native breeches. Elsa and her aunt both gasped at the sight of him in his unusual garments, and then they pretended to ignore him.

Mrs. Taft spoke up, "Come on in, Uncle Ned. I would like you to meet these ladies."

Uncle Ned stepped forward, and Mrs. Taft introduced him to Frau Schiller and Elsa Wagner. Both women were distant and very formal with the old man.

They probably can't figure out exactly who he is, Mandie thought as she watched.

When the Cherokee finally sat down, Mandie rushed to grasp his hand and say goodnight. And as the conversation began again among the adults Mandie whispered, "Did you see Rupert anywhere outside?"

Uncle Ned shook his head and said softly, "No see him."

Mrs. Taft glanced at her granddaughter and said, "Amanda! Bedtime, dear."

"Yes, Grandmother," Mandie replied.

The three young people bid everyone goodnight and left the room to go upstairs.

After they were out of hearing, they paused to make their plans.

"Let's meet at the top of the stairs as soon as everyone has gone to bed," Mandie said softly to her friends.

"Are you sure you really want to go outside in the dark and watch the tree?" Celia asked. "It may be too dark to see anything."

"Celia, if you don't want to come you don't have to,"

Mandie said indignantly. "It'll be all right if you just want to go to bed. Jonathan will go with me, won't you, Jonathan?"

"Sure, I wouldn't miss this for anything," Jonathan said with his mischievous smile.

"No, Mandie, I really do want to go, because the tree may jump up and down and I don't want to miss that," Celia replied as they all moved on up the stairs.

"All right," Mandie agreed. "I doubt that we'll see the tree jump up and down, but we'll go watch just in case."

The three went to their rooms, agreeing to listen for the occupants of the house to retire. Then they would meet at the top of the stairs for their adventure outside.

When Mandie opened the door to her suite, Snowball jumped down from a nearby table and came running to his mistress, meowing for all he was worth. She picked him up.

"You missed me, didn't you, Snowball?" Mandie said, cuddling the kitten on her shoulder and rubbing his white fur. He kept wailing.

"Mandie, something must be wrong with him, crying like that," Celia said, going to look at him.

Mandie held him in her arms to look at him. "What is wrong, Snowball?" She quickly ran inside the bathroom and looked around for his food bowl. There was no dish anywhere.

"Oh, goodness! Olga must have forgotten to feed Snowball!" Mandie said with a big sigh.

"No wonder he is crying then," Celia said.

"I suppose I'll have to go back downstairs and look for the kitchen to get something to eat for him," Mandie decided, putting Snowball down.

"Want me to go with you?" Celia asked.

"All right, but let's be awfully quiet so no one will hear

us. Otherwise, Grandmother may find out we've been prowling around the castle when we're supposed to be going to bed," Mandie said.

The two girls went softly along the corridors and down the stairs. Then they explored different directions and finally found themselves in the hallway on to which the old kitchen opened.

"That door goes into that old kitchen, I think, so we must be near the kitchen they use now," Mandie whispered as she went toward the closed door.

She carefully pushed open the door enough to see inside, with Celia peeking over her shoulder. Both girls gasped as they watched Rupert lower something on a rope into the old well inside the room. He bent over to watch it go down. Then he leaned forward over the edge, apparently tying the end of the rope to something down below. He straightened up, smiled to himself, and brushed his hands together.

The girls quickly darted down the corridor to the nearest door and ran inside of what was evidently the pantry. They listened quietly as Rupert walked heavily down the hallway until his footsteps could no longer be heard.

Mandie whispered, "Let's go see what he put in that well." She was out of the pantry and hurrying to the old kitchen before Celia could object.

The girls examined the well, and although there was only one dim lamp burning in the room, they could see the hook far, far below where the rope was secured.

"No way we can reach that," Mandie said, exasperated.

"No, we might fall in," Celia cautioned.

"If we could find a long stick, we might be able to pull on the rope," Mandie suggested.

"Mandie, it's too late to mess with that," Celia objected. "Remember, we have to get food for Snowball and then we are going outside to watch the tree."

"Yes, you're right, Celia," Mandie said, straightening up. "Tomorrow we'll look to see if the rope is still down there. Now let's find the kitchen."

The girls discovered the present-day kitchen was just next door. They heard laughter behind the door and pushed it open. The servants were busy cleaning. They all stopped to look at the girls in the doorway.

"Could we please have some food for my kitten?" Mandie asked as she and Celia stepped into the room.

The three uniformed women servants looked at her and then at one another.

"Oh, goodness, Mandie, they don't understand English," Celia said.

"Food," Mandie repeated, putting her fingers to her mouth. Then she crooked her arms and said, "Kitty, kitty, kitty."

The women exchanged glances again and then laughed, still not comprehending.

Mandie walked over to the leftover food on the long wooden table, picked up a used dish and pointed with it toward the food.

"Ah!" the oldest woman said with a big smile. She reached into a cupboard, took out a small bowl and went to the big iron stove across the room. There were several pots, and she lifted the lid on the largest and dipped inside with a large ladle.

Mandie followed her and watched. Evidently this was part of the stew they had had at dinner. Snowball would love it.

"Not too full. I might spill it," Mandie said as the woman kept filling the bowl.

Not understanding Mandie's remark, the woman ignored her and reached back into the cupboard, pulled out a large dish towel and covered the bowl with it. Then she handed it to Mandie with a burst of German words and a smile.

"Thanks," Mandie said. Then she remembered the expression Jonathan had translated when they overheard Frau Schiller. She repeated the German word: "Danke."

All three women smiled broadly, and watched the girls as they left the room.

Mandie carefully balanced the bowl as they made their way back to their rooms.

Snowball greeted them with more wailing until Mandie set the bowl on the bathroom floor. He immediately gobbled down the stew.

"You eat your fill, and then you climb up on the bed and go to sleep," Mandie told her cat as she and Celia went back into the bedroom to sit on the big bed.

"I wonder what Rupert put in that well. We've just got to find out," Mandie remarked.

"Maybe Jonathan could reach it," Celia suggested.

"Good idea. We'll tell him about it when we go outside in a little while," Mandie agreed. "And I do hope this venture will be worthwhile, because I imagine it is cold out there."

"Me, too," Celia agreed. "Germany is much colder this time of year than back home."

"Let's get our cloaks ready," Mandie said.

They prepared their wraps, and sat quietly waiting until they thought it would be late enough for everyone to have gone to bed.

Chapter 8 / What Has Rupert Been Doing?

"It's time," Mandie said softly as the clock struck midnight somewhere in the castle. She picked up her dark heavy cloak and put it around her.

Celia did likewise. "Are we going to leave Snowball here?" she asked.

"Definitely," Mandie replied, looking at the ball of white fur sleeping on the bed.

Mandie slowly opened the door and looked out into the hallway. There was no one in sight. "Come on," she whispered.

Celia followed, carefully closing the door to their suite.

The deep silence and the dim lights in the wide corridor made the place eerie. The girls crept along slowly, careful not to make any noise. Mandie held her breath, hoping no one would appear and catch them up after hours. She was determined to watch the tree.

When they finally got to the landing of the stairs, they

found Jonathan sitting on the top step. He grinned and rose as they came up.

"I'm ready," he told them in a low voice.

"So are we," Mandie said.

They softly descended the huge staircase, pausing now and then to listen for any sound. The front door came into view at the far end of the corridor downstairs and the three hurried toward it.

As they drew nearer, Mandie suddenly put out her hands to stop her friends. She had spotted Rupert sitting on the bench by the door where they had sat earlier watching the arrival of Elsa Wagner and Frau Schiller. Celia and Jonathan saw him at the same time. He seemed to be reading some papers on the table.

The three young people quietly, slowly, backed up the hallway, keeping an eye on Rupert, and stepping into an adjoining corridor.

"Now how will we get out of here?" Mandie asked in a whisper.

"We'll just find another door," Jonathan said in a low voice.

"The only other door I know of is the one near the old kitchen—which reminds me," Mandie whispered. "Jonathan, we saw Rupert putting something down the well in that old kitchen. We had to go find something for Snowball to eat because Olga had not fed him. He was meowing like he was starved. We happened to find the old kitchen while we were looking for the one they use now."

"Something into the well?" Jonathan questioned. "What did it look like?"

"We couldn't tell," Celia spoke up.

"We only saw him let the rope down in the well with something on the end of it," Mandie explained. "Then he tied the top end of the rope so far down we couldn't reach it to pull it up, but I think you could."

"Let's go see," Jonathan agreed in a low voice.

The three quietly made their way to the old kitchen. Mandie softly pushed open the door, enough to peek in. There was no one inside.

"Come on," she said, stepping into the old kitchen and going to the well.

Mandie explained to Jonathan about the rope. He looked down inside the well.

"I can see the rope, but it seems to be fastened a long way down," Jonathan said, bending as far as he could.

"Can you reach it?" Mandie asked.

Jonathan tried and tried to make contact with the rope swinging inside the well, without any success. He straightened up to look at Mandie. "I'm not as tall as Rupert, you know. I can't reach as far as he can. But if I had something to hook on to the rope I could pull it up."

The three looked around the room without finding anything that could be used.

"What about something from the wall in the hallway? There's a lot of antique armor and tools hanging there," Mandie said.

"That's a good idea," Jonathan agreed. The three went out into the corridor.

Mandie spotted a long spear hanging over a doorway. "What about that thing?" she asked, pointing to it.

"Maybe we could find something lower, where we can reach it without climbing," Jonathan said, walking on to look at the various tools.

In a large alcove off the hallway was a huge open fireplace. Mandie found a poker standing beside it. She grabbed it and turned back to Jonathan.

"Here, this ought to do," she told him as he took the tool.

Jonathan examined the poker. "I believe it will," he said.

Back in the kitchen the girls watched as Jonathan lowered the poker into the well and tried to snatch at the rope. After a few tries he hooked it.

"I got it!" he exclaimed as he began to pull upward.

Mandie and Celia crowded near as he brought the rope out of the well. The end of it was tied to an old bucket. But the bucket was empty.

"Of all things!" Mandie exclaimed, examining the bucket. "I wonder why he put this bucket into the well. It's dry, which means it didn't go all the way down into the water."

"The well may be dry," Celia said.

"Of course!" Mandie agreed, as Jonathan began to lower the bucket back into the well. "It was probably used to draw up water when the well was in use."

Jonathan finished lowering the bucket. The top end of the rope was still attached to the hook where Rupert had tied it.

"I hear someone coming!" Mandie suddenly whispered.

The three looked around the room and found another door, which they quickly entered. Quietly peering out, they saw Rupert enter the old kitchen with the papers he had been reading. He rolled them up, tied a string around them, pulled the bucket up and put them in it. Then he lowered the bucket back into the well.

Mandie and the others watched as Rupert glanced around the room, and then left by the hall door through which he had come. The three breathed a collective sigh of relief. Mandie started to push the door open to go back into the old kitchen, when Rupert suddenly came back through the door from the hallway. The three withdrew quickly and peeked to see what Rupert was doing.

Rupert walked around the room several times, and then put out the one lamp burning there. Mandie had to squint to see him in the darkness as she watched through a crack in the door. Rupert withdrew the bucket from the well and removed the papers he had just put in it.

At that moment someone else entered the old kitchen. A woman with long dark hair.

"It's about time you got here," Rupert told her.

"I thought you were coming to my house in the woods," the woman replied.

"Didn't you find my note?" he asked as they stood there in the darkness.

"We've always met at my house. Therefore—" the woman began.

Rupert interrupted angrily, "You are aware that Elsa has arrived. I could not go visiting you while she is here."

"I know. Anyway, I finally thought to look in our secret hiding place to see if you had left any message," the woman said. "And I found your note there. I came as soon as I got it."

Mandie held her breath as she eavesdropped with her friends. Who was this woman? What was Rupert up to?

Rupert held up the papers in his hand and said, "I have everything signed here, and I want you to deliver these to Herr Zieger tonight. He will give you cash—a lot of money to bring back to me."

"But what are those papers?" the woman wanted to know. "And how am I going to find you when I get back?"

"These are legal papers," Rupert said, holding them out to her. "Now hurry on. I'll be here when you return."

"Legal papers? Will I get into trouble delivering them?

What is this all about?" the woman asked.

Rupert angrily smacked the palm of his hand with the rolled-up papers. "It is all legal," he said. "And if you must know, it covers property that I own, property that my dear American-loving mother gave to me before she ran off with that stupid American. I am selling it to spite her."

The woman gasped. "Are you certain I won't be involved in any trouble?" she asked. "I have my mother to take care of, which I won't be able to do if I am accosted by the law."

"Do not worry about the law," Rupert said impatiently as he handed her the papers. "You will have to take the pony cart. The amount of money will be too heavy to carry, even though Herr Zieger lives on the next property. I will wait for you in the library. Now, go!" He gave her a little push.

"All right, all right," the woman said, holding on to the papers as the two turned to leave the room.

"And be very quiet hitching up the cart," Rupert was saying as they closed the door behind them.

Mandie and her friends drew deep breaths as they continued to stand by the door.

"Well, so he hates Americans. And *we* are Americans," Mandie said.

"Yes," Jonathan agreed.

"And he is doing things to spite his mother," Celia added.

"We need to do something about that," Mandie said.

"We can't go interfering with Rupert's personal business, Mandie," Jonathan objected.

"But his grandmother ought to know what he's doing," Mandie said.

"Mandie, his grandmother doesn't speak English, so we can't even talk to her," Celia reminded her.

"Maybe I could learn enough German to explain to her," Mandie said.

"Never!" Jonathan told her. "I know a little German, but I could never learn enough in the few days we're going to be here to carry on a conversation with the baroness."

"Frau Jahn speaks both languages!" Mandie exclaimed. "I could talk to her and ask her to tell the baroness."

"I don't think the baroness would appreciate such personal business being discussed with her servants," Jonathan said.

"Well, I'll think of some solution," Mandie said, quickly turning to go down the corridor. "Come on. Let's go watch the tree. It may be already jumping by now."

The three found their way outside without seeing anyone. Mandie led the way around the castle to the juniper tree. The moon was shining brightly but the night air was cold. They found a low wall around a flower bed nearby, and they all sat down there to watch and wait.

Mandie's thoughts strayed to the scene they had just witnessed in the old kitchen. Who was that woman? She couldn't see the stranger very well in the darkness, but she was pretty sure she was not Yvette, the maid. Well then, she must be the woman they had seen in the cottage in the woods, because they had heard her refer to her house in the woods.

Turning to her friends, Mandie said, "You know, Rupert must know that woman awfully well to ask her to do something like he did and to carry a whole lot of money for him."

"She is probably a worker of some kind here at the castle," Jonathan said.

"Right, and I am pretty sure it wasn't Yvette," Celia spoke up. "The woman we saw didn't have a French accent like Yvette would."

"I wonder why they were talking in English, when we know Rupert hates Americans so much. You'd think he would refuse to use our language," Mandie remarked as she watched the tall juniper tree in front of them.

"Maybe that is the only language both he and the woman speak. The woman may not speak or understand German. You know she did have an unusual accent," Jonathan added.

As the three talked they kept their attention on the tree. Not even the wind was moving the branches of the giant juniper. The night was almost completely silent. Once in a while the sound of the horses drifted up to them, and insects twittered in the darkness.

Mandie pulled her dark cloak tighter around her. *How could that huge tree ever jump up and down*, she wondered as she gazed at it. Someone must be making up stories, but how could she prove them wrong? Unless she saw it with her own eyes she'd never believe that tale.

Turning back to her friends, she said, "I wonder where Elsa is. You'd think we'd see her somewhere in the house at least, but she seems to be staying in an isolated room somewhere in the castle."

Jonathan smiled his mischievous smile as he replied, "Rupert may have had something to do with that. He wouldn't want her too close around because of his other lady friends."

"Lady friends?" Mandie exclaimed. "You think he has lady friends?"

"Sure, he's old enough to be interested in women if he's old enough to be engaged," Jonathan said.

"We did see him at that cottage in the woods, and we heard him in the room with the maid," Celia agreed.

"Someone needs to straighten that young man out," Mandie said, vehemently stamping her foot. "Chasing other women when he's engaged, and selling land to spite his mother. I still think we ought to tell on him somehow, even if it would make him angry with us. He doesn't like us anyway."

"But, Mandie, we've been over all that already," Jonathan said. "Please don't insist on exposing his various activities. I won't join in on that."

"Neither will I," Celia spoke up.

Mandie sighed heavily and swished her cloak around her closer. "But we're supposed to help the wayward, and we'd certainly be helping him if we told on him, because I imagine the baroness would take some strict measures."

"We don't really know the baroness that well," Jonathan said. "She might take the view that we were meddling in her private affairs."

Horse's hooves clopped in the distance and the three young people immediately became quiet and listened and watched to see what was coming up the road. A small cart pulled by a pony came into view.

"It's that woman returning with the money," Mandie whispered.

"Right," Jonathan agreed.

"Let's be real quiet so she won't see us," Celia said, shrinking down into her dark cloak.

The cart went on down the driveway and around the castle. As soon as it was out of sight, Mandie jumped up and beckoned to her friends. "Let's go watch!" she told them.

They slipped silently around the end of the castle to where they could see the woman tying the pony to a hitching post. The woman looked around, tossed her long hair back and went through the doorway to the castle. The young people silently hurried after her, staying in the shadows, and then noiselessly entering the house. The woman was nowhere in sight.

"She was going to meet Rupert in the library. Do you know where that is?" Mandie whispered to Jonathan.

"I have an idea. Follow me," Jonathan replied.

"Please be quiet," Celia reminded them.

Jonathan led the way through corridors and doors until they finally spotted the woman walking ahead of them. They slowed down so she wouldn't see or hear them. She pushed open double doors on the corridor wall and went inside.

The young people rushed up to the doors as soon as they closed, and Mandie peeked through the large keyhole. She could see Rupert sitting in the room. He stood up as the woman approached him.

"Did you get the money?" he asked.

"No," the woman answered. "Herr Zieger is away for the night his butler said." She withdrew the rolled-up papers from under her cloak. "Here are your papers."

Rupert snatched them out of her hand and stamped about the room.

"If you had gotten here earlier you would have caught him before he left," Rupert told the woman. "But you had to be late meeting me, and by the time you got to his house, of course he was gone."

The woman stood there silently looking at Rupert.

Rupert stopped in front of her and said in an authoritative voice, "You be here tomorrow night by nine o'clock at the latest, do you understand? And I don't want any more excuses. Now go on home. I have to put these papers away."

Without a word the woman turned to leave the room. The young people scampered down the hallway and darted into a dark room. It seemed to be a small parlor. They pushed the door almost closed and watched as the woman left. She disappeared quickly down the corridor.

"Oh, he is mean!" Mandie said crossly.

"She must work for him or she would have said something back," Celia said.

"Or maybe she is in love with him," Jonathan teased as they watched for Rupert to leave the library.

"I don't see how anyone could love that mean man," Mandie said. Rupert came down the hall from the library. He was not carrying the papers with him. Mandie thought he must have hidden them in the library. He disappeared quickly.

"I suppose we might as well go to bed. It must be late," Mandie decided. "No use in looking for the papers in the library this time of night."

"But why would you want to look for Rupert's papers?" Jonathan asked.

"I'm just curious about what he is doing," Mandie replied, opening the door.

"But it's none of our business, Mandie," Celia said, following her into the hallway.

"I still think we might be able to help straighten him out somehow," Mandie insisted.

"Well, I am going to bed," Jonathan stated as he walked quickly ahead of the girls. "I see no sense in standing around all night discussing Rupert."

Mandie looked at him and sighed. "We stayed up this late and we still didn't see the tree jump."

The girls followed Jonathan upstairs to their suite.

Mandie couldn't get Rupert's activities out of her mind. He was really acting strangely. And someone ought to know about it.

Chapter 9 / The Dark-haired Woman

After breakfast the next morning, when the girls had gone back to their rooms, Olga asked Mandie if she would like to go with her to get the trunk from the attic.

"The dinner party tonight will keep us all busy," Olga said, placing a bowl of food in the bathroom for Snowball. "We should get that trunk for you this morning."

Mandie watched Snowball gobble up the food. "All right, but let me get Jonathan to go with us," she told the maid.

"Hurry, miss," Olga said. "Much work awaits me."

Mandie hurried into the hallway and knocked on Jonathan's door. He had already taken off his shoes to relax, but opened the door at once.

"We are going to the attic now," Mandie told him, smiling. "To get another trunk for me."

"Wait!" Jonathan replied with his mischievous smile. He darted back for his shoes. "I'm ready."

Jonathan pulled on his shoes as they returned to Mandie's room.

"All ready?" the maid asked as she led the way down the corridor.

"I shut Snowball in the bathroom," Celia told Mandie. "He wasn't finished eating."

"Good," Mandie said as they hurried along behind Olga. "I'll take him outside for fresh air later."

Mandie loved attics and she was anxious to see what was in the baroness's attic. *It's probably crammed full of antiques*, she thought as they went along. *But probably everything is dirty, broken, and jumbled.*

Olga led them down steps that ended in a huge courtyard. High stone walls surrounded it but there was no roof.

"What a place!" Mandie exclaimed as they followed Olga across the stone floor.

"I thought attics were supposed to be upstairs," Celia protested.

"Maybe they do things backward here," Jonathan teased.

"Oh, but we have to come down in order to go up," Olga turned back to explain. Crossing the open patio she entered a door, with the young people right behind her, and they found themselves in a hallway with steep stairs ascending before them.

"The castle must have been made in pieces," Mandie said as they looked around.

"That is true, miss," Olga said as she led them up the steps. "Added to after each occupant passes on. Every generation has their own ideas."

"Have you been working here long?" Mandie asked behind her.

"*Ja*, I was born here and my mother before me," Olga explained.

There were no floor breaks in the stairs, just steps going up, up, up, with a small landing now and then.

"Once you start up you can't get off these steps," Celia said, "except by going back down."

"That is correct," Olga said, as she hurried ahead.

Looking up at the steps that went almost out of sight above, Jonathan said, "Whew! After all this I may not be able to come back down."

"And there is no bannister to slide down on," Mandie said, laughing, as she looked at the small metal handrail.

Olga went up the steps so fast, that by the time the young people got to the top all three were almost out of breath. Mandie looked around when she reached the last step. They were in a circular room, wide open to the stairs. Small slits of windows high up on the wall barely illuminated the place. And as she looked closer she realized there was nothing but trunks and more trunks, all lined up in neat rows, and each one with a label attached. Each was numbered.

Celia and Jonathan paused too, surveying the room.

"Does the baroness keep only trunks in her attic?" Mandie asked in a puzzled voice.

"Only trunks in the trunk attic where we are. She has other attics for other things," Olga explained.

"Well, she certainly is a neat housekeeper, with everything all sorted out," Celia remarked.

"*Ja*," Olga replied, walking among the trunks. "All my life I see only sorted-out attics. Now, miss, which trunk would you like?" She turned to Mandie.

Mandie was not certain what to do, whether she should walk around and examine each trunk, or just point to one. She sighed and looked at Olga. "Why don't you pick one for me, as near the size of mine as possible so it will hold all of my things?"

"Oh, but there are several that size," Olga said, walking around the room. "Would you like this brown one, or that black one over there? Or maybe you would like the one in the corner with all the fancy brass hinges." She stood waiting for Mandie's answer.

Mandie quickly glanced at the trunks Olga indicated and then she said with a sigh, "I think I'll be fancy and take the one with the brass hinges, please."

Olga smiled, walked over to the trunk, and lifted the lid. Mandie and her friends followed. Inside was an elaborate framework for hanging garments and a tray for small items.

"You have made a good choice, miss," the maid said. She glanced at the label. "This trunk is number 100, the highest number here, which means it is the newest."

"Are you sure the baroness won't mind if I take one of her trunks?" Mandie asked as she straightened.

"I have explained to Frau Jahn and she has told the Baroness Geissler of your need. The baroness has given permission to take any trunk in this attic," Olga told her.

"Thank you," Mandie said. Turning to Celia, she asked, "Don't you think this one is pretty?"

"It looks awfully expensive, Mandie," Celia replied.

"Maybe I should break the lock on my trunk so I could get a nice one, too," Jonathan teased with his mischievous smile.

"Jonathan, I'd much rather have my own trunk, but since I can't lock it anymore I have to take this one," Mandie said seriously.

Jonathan started to pick up the end of the trunk and Olga said, "Nein, we get helpers to take the trunk down to the miss's suite. They have experience on the steps."

"That's right, Jonathan," Mandie said. "It would be some job for us to try to carry a trunk down those narrow, steep steps."

"Now we go," Olga said, turning to go down the stairs. "Today the helpers will put that trunk in your room, miss."

"Thank you, Olga, and if you will, please tell the baroness I appreciate it," Mandie said as they hurried down.

"*Ja*, I will," Olga replied.

Once they were all back inside the corridor to their suite, Olga left them to attend to her duties.

"I need to take Snowball outside for a while," Mandie told her friends. "And we can check on the juniper while we're out there if y'all want to."

Jonathan and Celia agreed and waited in the hallway while Mandie went to put Snowball on his leash.

As the three walked around the backyard, Mandie happened to see Ludwig, the jockey. He was coming up a path toward the house. Mandie waved to him and he smiled back, then stopped to speak to them.

"Would you have time to show us the horses now, Herr Ludwig?" Mandie asked.

"Of course, miss," the jockey said with a smile and a small bow. "I am at your service anytime. It would be a pleasure to show you young Americans the baroness's horses." He looked at Jonathan and Celia.

"Oh, yes, please," Celia said excitedly.

"I would be interested in seeing them, too," Jonathan added.

"Then we must go visit them," Ludwig said, turning back down the pathway he had come. "It is a nice little walk."

Ludwig led them down the path that meandered through open fields and then through dense woods, until finally they came into an opening and saw dozens of thoroughbreds.

Celia broke from the group and ran to the fence. Her family had raised horses for generations back home in Virginia and she dearly loved the animals. She leaned on the rail, gazing about. Mandie tied Snowball to a bush away from the fence in case the horses didn't like him.

The others came up behind her and Ludwig whistled slightly. One of the young horses came to him at the fence. The animal nuzzled his hand between the rails. Then the horse turned to Celia, who was thrilled with the attention.

Mandie had her own pony back home and was an expert rider, but she didn't have the rapport with the animals that Celia did.

"Aren't they beautiful?" Mandie exclaimed as she stood beside Celia, who was talking gibberish to the attentive horse.

Jonathan was plainly impressed with the horses. "I wish my father would move out of New York into the country somewhere so I could own a horse," he said wishfully.

Mandie quickly turned to him and said, "Maybe he will. Senator Morton seems to think your father will be a changed man when you return home. He thinks your father realizes now how he has neglected you."

Jonathan dropped his gaze and kicked at the bottom rail of the fence. Then he looked up at Mandie with a big grin and laughing, he said, "I don't really want him to change completely, just enough to have some time with me so I can really get to know him."

"Does he ride?" Mandie asked.

"I don't even know," Jonathan replied. "I suppose he does. He spends a lot of time with friends in upstate New

York on their country estates."

"Then I would imagine he does," Mandie decided.

They turned back to the fence to watch the horses. Then a loud voice suddenly spoke behind them. They whirled around to see Rupert standing there. "I see you Americans are enjoying our horses," he said as he came up to the fence beside Ludwig.

Celia smiled at him, and said breathlessly, "Oh, yes."

Mandie was instantly on the defensive, wondering what he was up to this time. She watched him closely, as did Jonathan.

Ludwig spoke up, "Are you looking for me?"

"Oh, no," Rupert said. "I'm waiting for my horse to be saddled at the barn. I'm going for a ride."

Mandie couldn't believe her ears when she heard Celia ask, "Could we go riding with you, Rupert?"

"Of course not. You wouldn't know how to handle our horses. After all, our horses don't understand your language," Rupert said with a sneer.

Celia gasped and looked at Mandie.

"I would imagine my friend Celia here could outride you anytime, no matter what nationality the horse is," Mandie said sharply.

Rupert pressed his lips together, looked at her, and then replied, "If that remark was meant to goad me into letting you people ride our horses it didn't work." He turned and walked away quickly up the path.

"Please forgive his manners," Ludwig said quickly. "He does not own the horses, they belong to the baroness. And if you'd like, I will ask if you could ride them."

"No, thank you. He has taken all the pleasure out of it," Celia said sadly.

"I don't think my grandmother would want us riding unfamiliar horses anyway," Mandie said.

"If you change your minds, please let me know and I will talk to the baroness," Ludwig told them.

"Thank you," Mandie said.

"We appreciate your kindness," Celia added.

"I wonder why Rupert doesn't seem interested in his fiancee," Jonathan said to the jockey. "Evidently he is going riding alone."

"It is an arranged marriage, and he doesn't like being told what to do, not even by the baroness. But the *fraulein* has the money needed to keep this place going, and Rupert will have the title someday," Ludwig explained. "An even swap, you might say." He smiled.

"I sure hope it all works out," Mandie said. She thought of her mother and father, whom her grandmother had managed to separate when she was born. Her father was half Cherokee, and Mrs. Taft wanted no Indian-blooded grandchildren. But things had finally changed for the good.

"He is going for a ride at an odd time. The noon meal is probably being put on the table right now," Ludwig said.

"Oh, goodness, we need to hurry!" Mandie exclaimed. "Thank you." She rushed back to the bush, untied Snowball, and picked him up.

"Can you find the way back? I'll be glad to walk back with you if you can't," Ludwig offered.

"We were only on one path. Even I can find the way back," Jonathan teased the girls, smiling at Ludwig.

"There are two small intersections, but just stay on the main pathway and you'll be all right," Ludwig cautioned.

After thanking him, the three began their walk back to the castle. They discussed Rupert's behavior, and when they came to the first intersection Rupert startled them by suddenly, and dangerously, riding across their path. They froze in their tracks. Then the woman they had seen the night before in the old kitchen came flying after him on another horse. The two riders ignored them and kept going.

"I think we ought to tell someone about the way Rupert has been acting," Mandie said, stamping her foot and holding tightly to Snowball, who was protesting loudly.

"Oh, Mandie, we don't want to be tattletales," Jonathan told her.

"We don't have anyone we can tell anyway, remember?" Celia reminded her friend.

"I'll figure something out," Mandie promised, walking ahead. "But we'd better hurry right now."

When the three young people entered the front door of the castle, they met up with Frau Jahn. She had been looking for them.

"The food is ready to put on the table," Frau Jahn said, reaching for Snowball. "I will take him and feed him." Mandie handed him to the housekeeper. "You don't have time to stop. I'll show you the way to the parlor."

The three found all the adults in the parlor. Frau Jahn spoke rapidly in German to the baroness and then disappeared down the hallway with Snowball in her arms.

The baroness smiled at the young people and waved her hand toward some chairs nearby. They sat down. Mrs. Taft sat with Senator Morton on a settee, and Uncle Ned stood at the window looking out. Then he came to join the group.

Upon seeing her old Cherokee friend, Mandie immediately decided she would talk to Uncle Ned about Rupert. Maybe he could help in some way. As soon as she could possibly get a chance alone with him, she would relate everything that had happened concerning Rupert.

Mrs. Taft spoke to them, "I'm glad to see you all got here in time to eat. No one knew where y'all were."

"I'm sorry, Grandmother," Mandie said. "We went for a walk and ran into the jockey, and he showed us the horses. They're absolutely beautiful!"

Mrs. Taft smiled at her. So did Senator Morton.

"Good horses!" Uncle Ned enthusiastically agreed, with a smile at Mandie.

Frau Jahn returned to the parlor then, and after speaking to the baroness she announced that they were ready to go into the dining hall.

As they walked along the corridor behind the adults, Mandie suddenly remembered Elsa Wagner and her aunt, Wilhelmina Schiller. She whispered to her friends, "Where are the other guests?"

Celia and Jonathan both looked at her and shook their heads.

Mandie's question was answered when they met the other guests at the dining hall door. Elsa was still wearing a dark dress and her aunt had on the same black dress. As Mandie listened to the conversation among the adults, she learned that Elsa and her aunt had been shopping in the village that morning for items they had forgotten to bring. Rupert was not present.

The dinner party scheduled for that night was the topic of conversation at the table. Elsa and her aunt seemed to limit their remarks to the adults, ignoring the young people.

"You young people must get some rest this afternoon," Mrs. Taft insisted. "The dinner tonight may be late breaking up, and the baroness would like you three to attend, including a late-night snack."

"Thanks, Grandmother," Mandie replied from across the table. "I was afraid we'd have to just eat the meal and then go to bed, and we'd miss out on all the doings after dinner."

"The doings, as you call it, will include a well-known soprano who will sing for us, and a small elite symphony will play after dinner," her grandmother explained.

"And I believe the baroness plans to have a magician perform later," Senator Morton added.

"A magician?" Mandie questioned. "Could it be the one we met in Rome?"

"Of course not, dear," Mrs. Taft said. "This man is German. Now, rest time this afternoon will be for one full hour, but I will allow you three to work out what time you take it."

"Yes, Grandmother," Mandie replied, and turned to her friends who were seated on either side of her. "We could stay in our rooms from three to four o'clock this afternoon. What do you think?"

"Fine," Celia agreed, between sips of coffee.

"That's all right with me," Jonathan said, his mouth full of potatoes.

Mandie looked across the table at Uncle Ned and said, "If you are not busy after four o'clock, could I please talk to you, Uncle Ned?"

The old Indian smiled and said, "Papoose talk any time."

"Then I'll meet you at the bench by the fountain in the front yard shortly after four," Mandie confirmed.

Jonathan and Celia looked sharply at her.

Mandie could tell they knew what she wanted to talk to Uncle Ned about, and they didn't think she should. Well, so be it! She was going to discuss Rupert's behavior with her Cherokee friend, and maybe he could figure out some way to help the young man. He was always able to solve a problem for her. And she didn't care if her two friends didn't approve.

Chapter 10 / Mandie Wants to Tattle

After the noon meal the three young people went for a walk, and Rupert's name was not mentioned. At three o'clock they went to their rooms to rest, as Mrs. Taft had requested. But once in their suite, Mandie and Celia couldn't rest they were so excited about the dinner party that night.

Mandie had already decided to wear her beautiful blue silk dress and it was hanging ready. And Celia would be putting on her white silk dress, with dainty blue and pink flowers embroidered around the hem.

The girls flopped on the big bed because they had promised Mrs. Taft to rest. Snowball roamed about the rooms.

They kept hearing carriages arriving below, but their rooms were on an end of the castle and their windows only offered a view of the driveway as it wound around out of sight.

"I've counted ten carriages already!" Mandie exclaimed as they watched still another vehicle wind around the castle. "Do you think all these people are going to spend the night here?"

"Probably," Celia said. "But then when you think about it, this castle must have an awful lot of bedrooms."

"Yes, and I suppose rich people over here in Europe have overnight guests by the dozens," Mandie decided. "Since this castle is so far out in the country they have a long way to travel, too."

"And the dinner party must be going to last way into the night, according to what your grandmother said. That will be fun. I've never been allowed to stay up late for such things at home," Celia remarked as they turned back to lie on the bed.

"My mother doesn't do much entertaining because of just having had my baby brother, I suppose," Mandie said. "My grandmother certainly is a social mixer, isn't she?"

"Well, yes, from what I have seen from being in her house in Asheville, when we attend school at Miss Prudence's," Celia replied. "And she also knows everyone. But, Mandie, your grandfather was a senator, and politicians always have a wide range of acquaintances."

"I wish I could have known my grandfather Taft, but he died many years ago," Mandie said. "I wonder what everyone back home is doing? My mother is probably still having to rock that crying baby. And Joe is probably visiting around with his father when Dr. Woodard makes his calls. And Uncle John is sure to be home tending to business. My life has certainly changed since April of last year when my father passed on."

"Mine has too, Mandie," Celia replied. "I lost my father, too. But just think of all the friends we've made. If you and I hadn't gone to the same school, we might never have met. And if we hadn't gone to that particular school, we never would have met up with Hilda."

"Or April Snow," Mandie added with a frown. "I wonder what she's doing this summer. Probably concocting some trick to play on us when we get back to school."

The girls talked on and on, and the first thing Mandie knew the small clock on the mantelpiece struck four. She jumped up from the bed and smoothed her skirts.

"It's time to go meet Uncle Ned," she said, looking in the mirror to brush back some loose blonde tendrils. "Celia, I won't be gone long. When I come back we could go watch the juniper tree, if you and Jonathan want to."

"All right," Celia agreed as she sat up and began straightening her long skirts. "I'll just stay here and play with Snowball. I'll also ask Jonathan if he wants to go."

"Thanks," Mandie said.

She hurried down into the yard and found her old Cherokee friend waiting on the bench by the fountain as they had planned. He motioned for her to sit by his side.

"Uncle Ned, this is a strange place, more so than any other place we've stayed at on our journey to Europe," Mandie began, looking solemnly up into his wrinkled face.

"Strange?" Uncle Ned questioned.

"Yes, you see, Rupert—the baroness's grandson—acts awfully strange," Mandie said, and she related the events concerning Rupert.

Uncle Ned listened intently as Mandie went into every detail.

"I wanted to ask you if you can figure out some way we can help him," Mandie said. "I think the baroness ought to know about his capers, especially about what he's doing with the property his mother gave him."

Uncle Ned shook his head and said, "Not Papoose's business. Must not meddle in others' business."

"But he needs help, help to show him how wrong he is, and help to get over his hatred of Americans," Mandie insisted. "If we could talk to the baroness, with Fran Jahn's help, of course, I believe she would see to it that he gets straightened out, because obviously she dearly loves him."

"No, no, Papoose must not be tale-tattler," he insisted as he reached to hold her small white hand in his dark one. "The only thing Papoose can do is ask Big God to help Rupert. Big God helps when no one on this earth can. And Papoose must stay away from Rupert, not watch him all the time."

Mandie felt let down.

She had thought Uncle Ned would help her solve Rupert's problem. And now he was saying pray and stay away from Rupert. Well, she would do that, but she would not give up trying to find other ways to get to Rupert.

She went back to her suite, and rather than let Celia know Uncle Ned had agreed with Celia and Jonathan about staying out of Rupert's business, she didn't say a word about her conversation with Uncle Ned.

"Ready?" she asked Celia as she entered the room where Celia was throwing a ball for Snowball to chase.

Celia straightened up and said, "Sure. Jonathan wants to go. I'll just knock on his door and let him know we're ready."

Jonathan joined the girls in the hallway. Mandie led Snowball on his red leash and the three went outside to sit and watch the juniper tree.

"That tree is never going to move," Mandie insisted as they sat on the low wall nearby. Snowball's leash was tied to a bush.

"Then why do you keep coming back to watch it?" Jonathan said. "I could think of lots of other things better to do than watching a forty-foot tree," Jonathan said.

"Like what?" Mandie asked.

"Like trying to find out where all these people are who have arrived for the dinner party tonight," Jonathan said. "I counted twenty-three carriages, but I haven't seen a single soul."

"Well, then where did they go?" Mandie asked. "They have to be inside the castle somewhere."

"But the castle is enormous, and the baroness has probably put them all the way to another end from where we're staying," Celia remarked.

"What do you want to do? Go roam around inside the castle?" Mandie asked, looking at the giant juniper tree. She had about given up on seeing it move.

"Why don't we roam around the grounds first and look for all the carriages that have come? They've got to be parked somewhere," Jonathan said as he rose.

"But the people are not in the carriages now," Mandie protested.

"I know, but some of the carriages may have names or family crests on them," Jonathan explained, and with his mischievous smile he added, "We might find out if anyone really important is here."

"Oh, my, Jonathan, but you sound like my grandmother," Mandie said with a laugh as she took Snowball's leash from the bush. "She always wants to know important people."

"The baroness has invited some Americans, remember? And there just might be someone here that we know or have heard of," Jonathan said with a laugh.

"Well, come on, let's go," Mandie said.

"We could ask Frau Jahn if she'd let us see the guest list," Celia suggested as they walked around the castle to the pathway that led to the outbuildings.

"And she might ask what business that is of ours, Celia," Mandie said. Snowball bounced along at the end of his leash.

"You're right," Celia agreed.

As the three came alongside a huge barn with several doors and windows, Mandie paused to look inside through the windowpane.

"Looks like tools in that part," Mandie murmured as she squinted to see inside. Then she quickly stepped back and motioned to her friends. "Rupert just came in and he's with that dark-haired woman," she whispered.

The three stayed behind the bushes growing by the window and eavesdropped as they tried to see inside.

"I do not care what you say, I am going to that dinner party tonight. You owe me that much," the woman was saying loudly.

"You are not doing any such thing," Rupert said angrily. "You know very well that Elsa is here. Besides, there are lots of people invited who might know who you are."

"I do not care," the woman insisted. "There is nothing you can do to stop me. I am going to the party."

Rupert took her by the shoulders and shook her. "No, you are not. Your presence would create havoc."

The woman withdrew from his grip and said, "Unless you agree, I will tell those Americans what you did."

The three young people's ears perked up.

"You do, and it will be the last thing you ever do," Rupert said firmly.

"I may not have to tell them myself," the woman said. "Unless you pay Herman for wrecking their carriage, he may tell on you himself."

Mandie gasped and the others looked at each other. *So Rupert was the cause of the accident!*

"He's not going to tell anyone," Rupert said. "It's worth too much money to him to keep silent."

"But you haven't paid him all the money you promised, and he is getting impatient," the woman reminded him.

"That's because I haven't been able to catch Herr Zieger to close out the deal on my property. You know that, and Herman knows that. Now get back home where you belong and do not show up here tonight, because if you do you may regret it," Rupert repeated indignantly.

"You will see," the woman said, rushing from the room. Rupert followed. The three young people had to sit on the ground behind the bushes to prevent Rupert and the woman from seeing them as they rushed out of the barn. As they peeked through the shrubbery they saw the woman mount a horse tethered nearby and take off like a streak of lightning. Rupert watched and then walked toward the castle.

"Rupert is a mean man!" Mandie said with a big sigh. "I think we should at least tell Grandmother that he paid that driver to wreck our carriage. We could have all been killed."

"You're right, we could have all been killed, but what good will it do to tell your grandmother? I'm sure she's not going to relay the message to the baroness that her grandson had our carriage wrecked," Jonathan said.

"She might," Mandie insisted. "Anyway, I think we ought to just pack up and leave this place. I believe that's what Grandmother would do if we told her about Rupert."

"We can't pack up and leave, Mandie," Celia said. "The baroness is having that dinner party tonight, and we are her guests, remember?"

"Yes, and we do want to be present to see if that woman has the nerve to show up after Rupert threatened her," Jonathan said.

"Oh, well, y'all are two against one so I guess you win," Mandie said with a sigh. "I won't go straight to tell Grandmother, but I won't promise that I won't tell her sometime or other, if the occasion comes up that seems to require it."

The three stood and continued their walk down the pathway. Eventually they came to a large lake in the middle of a dense stand of trees.

"Look! A lake!" Mandie exclaimed, rushing to the edge of the water to look.

"Not so close, Mandie. You can't swim, remember?" Celia warned her friend.

"I know that," Mandie replied. "But this is a surprise, finding a lake this big on the baroness's property."

"I suppose this is still her property down here," Jonathan remarked.

A voice behind them startled them, and they turned around to see Rupert standing there.

"Of course this is my grandmother's property, and I would not advise you to go swimming in it. It is very deep," Rupert said with a smirk. He turned to Mandie and added, "And you can't swim, eh?"

"We are not planning to go swimming anywhere, Rupert," Mandie told him. "So it doesn't matter whether I can swim or not, do you understand?"

"I understand you cannot swim," Rupert replied, quickly turning to go back up the pathway.

The three young people stood there silently watching until he disappeared from their sight.

"Oh, he's always snooping on us," Mandie said, stamping her foot, which caused Snowball to meow and jump around at the end of his leash.

"And we're always snooping on him. Fair enough?" teased Jonathan.

"But he *needs* to be snooped on," Mandie protested. "Anyhow, let's go back to the castle."

"And walk around inside to see if we can find any of the other guests," Celia added.

The three young people roamed around the corridors of the castle, opening doors here and there, until they finally found themselves in another section. Everyone else seemed to be staying there. They met up with several nicely dressed ladies going down the hallways and some of the doors were open. They could see the occupants inside. Everyone they saw looked rich and well-dressed, Mandie decided.

No one paid the young people any attention until they arrived at the end of a long corridor and passed the last door, which stood wide open. A beautiful young girl about Mandie's age was sitting on a settee looking out into the hallway. When she heard the three talking in the hallway, she jumped up and came to the doorway.

"Oh, you must be the other American guests," the girl exclaimed in an American accent. "I haven't found any other Americans to talk to. Have you?"

"No, we haven't seen any others that we could identify as Americans," Mandie replied, staring at the girl's elaborate hairdo and her expensive red silk dress, which set off her dark curls. She had dark eyes and long black lashes.

Jonathan spoke up, "You are from New York, right?" He smiled knowingly.

"Well, how did you know?" the girl asked with a gasp. "Yes, I am from New York. My name is Dorothy McSwain. What's yours?"

"I am also from New York," Jonathan replied with a grin. "That's how I know the accent when I hear it. My name is Jonathan Guyer and these are my friends, Mandie Shaw, from North Carolina, and Celia Hamilton, from Virginia."

"I am so glad to meet all of you," the girl said in a bubbly voice. "I came with my father, and he has already gone off somewhere and left me here to rest up for the dinner party, but I can't rest when there's so much going on."

"Neither can we," Mandie replied as they stood there in the doorway. Snowball cavorted at the end of his leash. "We're making our own tour of the castle. Want to come along?"

"Oh, definitely," Dorothy said. "Just let me hang up this dress I had pressed for tonight." They watched as she picked up a frothy pink dress from a chair and hung it on a peg on the end of the huge wardrobe. "There. Now I'm ready." She came into the hallway and closed the door behind her.

"Let's go this way. We haven't been down this hall," Mandie said, leading the way into a cross hallway. The others followed. Mandie found the girl was taller than she was and she had to look up a little to talk to her. "Have you been here before?"

"Never," Dorothy replied. "But my father has, many times. And the baroness and Rupert have visited us in New York."

"And they have visited my father in New York when I was away at school," Jonathan told her.

"So you know Rupert," Mandie said.

The girl laughed and said, "Yes, I know Rupert. I know a little too much about Rupert."

"So do we," Celia spoke up.

"Did you know that he is engaged to marry Elsa Wagner, and that she and her aunt, Madam Schiller, are here?" Mandie asked.

"I knew he was engaged," Dorothy said as they walked along. "But I didn't know his fiancee is here. I met Elsa when she came to New York. I don't think she really wants to marry Rupert."

The three stopped and looked at Dorothy.

"She doesn't?" Mandie asked. "We don't think Rupert wants to marry her, either."

"He doesn't?" Dorothy exclaimed. "Then why are they getting married?"

"We understand it was all arranged," Mandie went on. "Rupert will inherit the title one day, and evidently the baroness can use Elsa's money to preserve this place." She watched the girl's reaction.

Dorothy frowned and said, almost angrily, "Money, money, money! That's all some people think of. And over here in Europe, it's titles, titles, titles! Thank goodness my father is not like that. He has plenty of money, but he couldn't care less about it."

"I would never, never marry anyone I didn't love," Mandie replied vehemently. "Money could not buy me."

"If neither one wants to marry the other, maybe the engagement will break up, especially with what we know about Rupert," Celia said.

"What do you know? Tell me, please," Dorothy insisted.

Celia looked at Mandie and didn't reply. Mandie frowned thoughtfully.

Jonathan answered the girl's question, "We don't have to tell you. Just wait till the dinner party tonight and watch for the fireworks."

"Now you really have me curious," Dorothy said. "Please explain what you're talking about."

"Sorry, we promised not to discuss Rupert," Mandie said. "But you'll see tonight."

"I'll tell you what I know about Rupert, if you'll tell me what you know," Dorothy offered.

The three young people looked at each other and shook their heads.

"I'm sorry," Mandie said, and quickly changed the subject. "Have you heard the tale about the juniper tree here?"

"The juniper tree? What about it?" Dorothy asked anxiously.

"Well, it's like this," Mandie began, and she told the story she had heard about the tree.

Dorothy was impressed, and begged to be allowed to sit and watch it with them the next time they did. "Please let me know when you go out to watch it."

"It's too near the time we should get ready for to-night," Mandie said. "But we'll let you know when we go out again. We'd better go back to our rooms and dress."

"Me, too," Dorothy agreed, and they went their separate ways at the intersection of the corridors.

Mandie called back to the girl, "Just remember to watch for the fireworks tonight!"

Dorothy waved back.

Mandie wondered what would really happen if the girl with the dark hair showed up after Rupert had warned her not to. She was looking forward to some excitement.

Chapter 11 / Uninvited Dinner Guest

Mandie and Celia excitedly dressed in their rooms for the dinner party. They helped each other put their hair up, and by the time they were finished they looked like two young ladies, rather than two thirteen-year-olds who were always into some adventure.

Whirling before the long mirror in the bedroom, Mandie exclaimed, "I think I look pretty good!" She giggled. "But it's only temporary, I suppose. Tomorrow I'll be back down to earth."

Celia surveyed herself beside Mandie. "Yes, we do look grown-up, don't we? I wonder what Elsa will wear. Dorothy's dress was sure pretty."

"I can guarantee you their dresses aren't any more expensive than ours, the way my grandmother and your mother spent money on our clothes for this trip," Mandie replied, tucking in a wisp of blonde hair that was already straying. "But then, money doesn't amount to a hill of beans to me. I think a person can look beautiful even in inexpensive clothes." She perched on the lid of the new trunk that had been sent down from the attic.

"Right," Celia agreed. She looked at her friend and added, "Don't you wish Joe could see you now?"

"Oh, but Joe doesn't care about finery. He's—he's— just plain old Joe, I guess you'd say," Mandie told her. "That's why I love him."

Celia stared at Mandie. "You love him?"

"Sure," Mandie replied with a slight blush. "I love him, and his father Dr. Woodard, and you, and Jonathan, and all my friends, don't you?"

Celia said with a smile, "Why, yes, I do. I even love Robert."

"Robert Rogers from Mr. Chadwick's back in Asheville?" Mandie asked.

"Of course," Celia said, still smiling.

"Oh, Celia, I didn't know," Mandie said excitedly. "Are you going to marry him when you grow up?"

"Mandie, that's many years away, and I hope to meet lots of other boys during that time. Who knows?" Celia replied.

There was a knock at the door. Mandie hastened to open it. Jonathan stood there in the latest fashion for young men.

Mandie teased, "Well, who are you?"

"And might I ask the same question? I was looking for Miss Shaw and Miss Hamilton, and here I find two beautiful young ladies in their rooms," Jonathan replied. "However, the substitutes will do just fine, if I may escort them to the drawing room."

Mandie and Celia giggled. Jonathan joined them. As their laughter subsided, Mandie caught her breath and said, "I can guarantee you I'd much rather be wearing my old calico and apron like I do back home, but then I would embarrass my grandmother among her wealthy friends."

"I like getting dressed up. It gives me self-confidence," Jonathan told her. "But come now, we don't want to be the last ones to enter the drawing room." He held out both arms.

Mandie quickly shut the door to her bedroom while Snowball was curled up asleep on the bed. She hoped Olga would bring him something to eat tonight.

With a girl on each arm, Jonathan found his way to the drawing room.

They might call it a drawing room, Mandie thought, *but it looks more like a huge ballroom.* The orchestra was already softly playing classical music. Guests were moving about, exchanging greetings.

"Do you see Rupert?" Mandie softly asked her friends as they looked about.

"No," Jonathan replied, shaking his head.

"I don't see anyone I know—your grandmother, Elsa and her aunt, or Uncle Ned. Well, yes, there is the baroness standing at the doorway down there," Celia said, pointing. "Apparently we were supposed to come in that door."

"That's all right," Mandie said. "We don't want to move along that long line of fancy strangers, do we?"

"But, Mandie, this dinner is given in honor of all the guests. We should do things right," Jonathan said.

"He's right, Mandie, let's go back out into the hallway and come in that door where the baroness is standing," Celia said.

"Well, all right," Mandie consented with a sigh.

At the other doorway the three found Mrs. Taft, Senator Morton, and Uncle Ned waiting for them. Dorothy was also there with a tall man who was evidently her father. She exchanged greetings with them.

"Amanda, I was afraid you'd be late, dear," Mrs. Taft said, turning to her granddaughter. "We must go through the line now. On your best behavior."

Mandie rolled her eyes at her friends as the three followed Mrs. Taft and Senator Morton through the doorway. There they found the baroness, Rupert, Elsa, and her aunt in the receiving line. Baroness Geissler spoke in German to them and Rupert quickly interpreted.

"My grandmother says she is honored to have you in her home and wishes you an enjoyable evening," Rupert said.

As Mrs. Taft and Senator Morton replied, Mandie was sure she heard Rupert add, "That doesn't include my wishes," under his breath as they moved along. She gave him a sharp glance and he tossed his head and looked the other way.

As they mingled with the crowd in the room, Senator Morton spoke to Jonathan, "I have checked on your relatives in Paris again. They have returned and immediately gone away on another assignment. They got our message, however, and responded that they would contact us when they return to Paris."

"Thanks, Senator Morton," Jonathan said with a smile. "Sooner or later I suppose we'll be able to communicate with them."

Dorothy joined them as the adults moved away. "I do believe we are the only young people in this crowd," she said.

The three looked around and Mandie said, "I think you're right. I'm so glad we met up with you."

"I am glad I met all of you," Dorothy replied. She was radiant in her bright pink dress that swept the floor. An air of confidence surrounded her. She was used to such social doings. "Jonathan, you promised fireworks at the dinner tonight. When does this happen?"

"Any minute," Jonathan said, with his mischievous smile. "Just keep your eyes and ears open and I'll let you know when."

The three young people kept a close watch on the crowd for the appearance of the dark-haired woman whom Rupert had forbidden to come to the dinner. Mandie saw Rupert moving about and speaking to various people here and there, but there was no sign of the woman—yet.

Before long the baroness led her guests into the great dining hall for dinner. Mandie noticed that there was plenty of room for all the many, many guests. She and her friends were seated alongside Dorothy, and Uncle Ned sat across the table from them. He wore the formal clothes that he had used for their visit to the White House for President McKinley's second inauguration. Mandie could sense that he was uncomfortable in such apparel, as she was also ill at ease in these gatherings of wealthy people that her grandmother took her and her friends to. She smiled at him and he smiled back.

The dinner seemed to go on for hours, until finally the baroness rose and asked her guests to return to the drawing room for entertainment. All four of the young people rose with a sigh of relief and followed the adults.

The well-known soprano (whom Mandie had never heard of) was already on the little stage at the end of the room, and as soon as everyone found a seat the woman began her rendition of old German songs. The young people fidgeted and looked about the room for any sign of the dark-haired woman. Everyone else seemed to be enjoying the music.

The orchestra played, and finally the magician performed for the guests. Mandie watched his every move, trying to catch on to his magic. The man did various tricks with handkerchiefs and balls and then he made an announcement.

"Ladies and gentlemen, I will now give you the highlight of the evening," he spoke in a loud voice. An assistant rolled a large trunk onto the stage, which stood on end, and the magician walked over to it and opened the lid.

The young people watched closely.

"You can see that this trunk is empty," he stated. He paused, walked around the stage and came back to the trunk. "I will now close the lid, and when I open it again you will see a beautiful young lady." He slammed it shut, waited a moment, shook a white handkerchief, and then reopened the lid.

The three young people gasped as the dark-haired woman Rupert knew stepped out of the trunk. She was wearing a beautiful gown of bright red silk, and sparkling gems at her throat and in her hair, which was piled high on her head. As the crowd clapped loudly she smiled, curtsied, and walked off the stage. The adults spoke to one another animatedly and shook their heads. The entertainment was finished for the night.

"That's the woman!" Mandie exclaimed.

Dorothy, sitting next to her, asked, "What woman? Do you know her?"

"She's the one who was to cause the fireworks tonight," Mandie whispered.

"I don't know about fireworks, but she is Lady Catherine," Dorothy stated.

Jonathan and Celia had leaned forward to listen. The crowd stood up and the young people did likewise.

"Lady Catherine?" Mandie asked.

"Yes, her family is from England. At one time they

were very wealthy, but now all she has is her title," Dorothy said.

"And Rupert treats her like a servant," Jonathan said.

Mandie quickly explained to Dorothy what they had seen. The girl listened in wonder at the tales of how Rupert had treated them.

"I had heard that Catherine intended to marry Rupert, one way or another," Dorothy told them as they moved about the room. "But, of course, the baroness will never allow it."

"Because she has no money?" Celia asked.

"That's right," Dorothy said. "Love doesn't mean a thing to people like the baroness. They make decisions with their accountant's advice, not listening to their hearts."

"I'm thankful my family is not like that," Mandie said.

"I wonder where she went when she left the stage. Let's see if we can find out," Jonathan suggested.

The four young people walked through the room behind the stage but found it empty. An outside door stood open at the back and they went into the yard. The surroundings were illuminated with dozens and dozens of lights, and many of the guests had also stepped outside, but the young people could find no sign of the woman, or of Rupert.

"I have an idea," Mandie said. "Remember the barn where we saw them earlier? Let's go look there."

As Mandie led the way down the lane, she explained to Dorothy about the barn. They had been looking for the parked carriages, and had found Rupert and Lady Catherine arguing in the barn.

"We never did find the carriages that all the people came in," Mandie said as they walked along, their skirts held up to avoid the dirt and weeds.

"Oh, I know where they are," Dorothy said. "Kurt, the baroness's head driver, supervised all that, and had them put in a clearing all the way across the field on the other side. My father happened to mention it because he had to go back to our carriage to get something he forgot."

They came within sight of the barn. Mandie cautioned everyone to be quiet just in case Rupert and the woman were there. The young people slowly made their way to the window of the barn and peeked in. A lantern partially illuminated the room, and to their amazement there was Rupert—holding Lady Catherine in his arms and kissing her!

"My goodness!" Mandie exclaimed, shyly backing away from the window. "Look at what Rupert is doing, and he's engaged!"

"I told you she was in love with him," Dorothy reminded them as they all looked inside and then cautiously moved away.

"Well, he must love her too, or he wouldn't be kissing her," Celia remarked in a soft voice.

"He's old enough to be in love," Jonathan said with his mischievous smile.

As they huddled there in the bushes, Mandie heard someone coming. "Sh-h-h! Someone is coming!" she whispered. The group remained motionless as they watched. A man in a dark cloak came swaggering down the pathway, went directly to the door of the barn and knocked loudly. The door immediately opened and Rupert stood in the doorway.

"I came for the rest of the money," the man said.

When he spoke, Mandie recognized him as the first driver of their carriage, the one who had wrecked it. She whispered this to her friends.

"I have repeatedly told you I will pay up when I can

close the deal with Herr Zieger," Rupert said angrily. "And I want you to stop bothering me about it."

"Then you stop that horseman, the one you asked me to hire to scare those people, from bothering me," the man said quickly. "He expects his pay from me, you know."

"I know, I know," Rupert replied. "And when I get the money I'll pay you." He started to shut the door, but the other man put his foot in to stop it.

"I'm only giving you till sundown tomorrow, or I'll go to the baroness herself," the man informed him.

"You try that and you'll never get your money," Rupert warned. "You dare to tell anyone anything and you'll wish you never had. Now go back where you belong."

The man withdrew his foot as he said loudly, "I mean business!" He walked off up the pathway, and Rupert slammed the door shut.

Mandie quickly explained to Dorothy what that was all about, and she was shocked that Rupert would enter into such a scheme.

"He is a very unstable person," Dorothy said vehemently. "I plan to steer clear of him."

"He is dangerous," Jonathan decided.

As the young people stayed hidden behind the bushes, Mandie thought she heard something again.

"I think there is someone else around here," she whispered to the others. They all remained very still and quiet, waiting to see if another person would appear on the pathway.

Mandie kept watching the dimly lighted window in the barn, even though from where they were they couldn't see Rupert and Lady Catherine inside. Suddenly a dark form materialized out of the darkness and moved over to stand in front of the barn window. The three young people gasped at once as the dim light from inside illuminated the face of the person.

"The woman from the ship!" Mandie exclaimed softly.

"Yes!" Jonathan and Celia both agreed.

Dorothy looked at them, not understanding.

"Let's approach her," Mandie dared her friends as she quietly stood.

"I'm with you!" Jonathan quickly assented.

Celia remained silent.

Mandie and Jonathan silently moved through the bushes toward the figure before the window. Just as they reached her, the woman turned and caught a glimpse of them.

"You are the lady from the ship!" Mandie spoke aloud. "What are you doing here?"

The woman replied in a low voice, "You will find out eventually!" Then she fled, vanishing in the darkness.

"Well, what do you suppose she was up to?" Mandie said impatiently, stamping her foot.

"Who was that?" Dorothy wanted to know.

The young people quickly explained to her about the woman watching them on the ship they had sailed on to London from the United States, and how she always seemed to turn up wherever they went. But they never could quite catch up with her to find out who she was and what she wanted.

Dorothy was excited. "That's a real mystery, isn't it? You must all lead such exciting lives, and nothing ever happens to me," she said with a sigh.

"Oh—something is going to happen right now," Mandie murmured as she turned to face Rupert and Lady Catherine standing there staring at them.

"What are you Americans doing here? The party is in the castle, in case you didn't know," Rupert said rudely.

"We know that very well, Rupert," Mandie told him. "We also know what you've been doing in that barn."

Rupert stepped toward her and said, "What I do is none of your business and you'd better not meddle in something that doesn't concern you."

Jonathan quickly stepped to Mandie's side. "But it does concern us," he said.

"Yes, we know now that you were involved in what happened to our carriage, and we could report it and make trouble for you," Mandie threatened.

"I don't know what you're talking about!" Rupert answered, balling up his fists.

Lady Catherine just stood there holding her breath as she listened and watched. Then she said, "Go ahead and tell everything. That would break up Rupert's engagement, which I would not be unhappy about."

Rupert gasped and said, "That is not the business of these nosey Americans! You had better go home, Catherine. Now!"

Lady Catherine stood there, smiling. "I'll go home when I want to and not before. I think I'd like something to eat or drink before I go, anyway. She turned toward the pathway to the castle. Rupert grabbed her arm to stop her. "Don't touch me." She moved away from him.

"Don't you dare go back to the castle," Rupert told her. "That silly act with the magician was enough, but if you go inside among our guests, I know my grandmother will insult you."

"Just because your grandmother doesn't want you to marry me doesn't mean that she would insult me," Lady Catherine insisted. "I'll go and see."

She turned and hurried up the pathway with Rupert right behind her. The young people followed.

"Here come the fireworks!" Mandie told Dorothy.

When Lady Catherine went through the doorway of the drawing room Rupert was still right behind her. The young people were close behind them. Several guests turned to look at the group. Then Mandie saw the baroness talking to her grandmother with Frau Jahn's help.

The four young people stopped to watch as Lady Catherine walked directly to the baroness. She turned to Lady Catherine without missing a breath, and extended her hand to the young woman. "How nice of you to join us, dear!" she said through Frau Jahn's interpretation.

Mandie and her friends were amazed, and Rupert stood with his mouth open.

"Rupert found me after I assisted the magician, and invited me inside for refreshments," Lady Catherine told the baroness through Frau Jahn. Baroness Geissler smiled at Lady Catherine, and Frau Jahn told the girl, "The baroness is delighted to serve you, and if you will follow me I will show you where the refreshments are."

Lady Catherine smiled at the baroness and followed Frau Jahn through the crowd. At the same time Mandie caught a glimpse of Elsa watching Lady Catherine. She wondered if Elsa had overheard the conversation.

Rupert quickly disappeared as the young people watched him.

Mandie turned to Dorothy and asked, "I wonder if you could tell me something. You seem to know all about Rupert and his grandmother. How can his last name be the same as his grandmother's if he is the son of her daughter?"

"That's common knowledge," Dorothy said. "His real father died when he was a child. The man had no money, no title, nothing, and the baroness had been against the marriage. So when he passed on, the first thing the baroness did was to legally adopt Rupert and change his name to hers so that he could inherit her title, property, everything."

"And then his mother married an American and moved to the United States," Jonathan added.

"And the baroness was glad, because then she would have Rupert all to herself. She worships the ground he walks on," Dorothy said.

"But she doesn't really know him," Celia remarked.

"Well, she may get to know all about him soon," Mandie said. "Lady Catherine may tell all."

"I hope she does," Jonathan said.

"And I hope we're around to find out about it," Mandie added.

Mandie was hoping Rupert would be exposed for what he really was. Maybe when his grandmother knew the truth, she would be able to help change him for the better. In the meantime, what was going to happen with Lady Catherine and Elsa? Who would win out?

Chapter 12 / What Made the Tree Jump

The next morning was cloudy. Mandie and Celia looked out their windows at the gray sky and sighed together.

"It's probably going to rain, and I wanted to watch that tree again today," Mandie moaned as she pulled her robe tightly around her.

"But it's not raining now," Celia said. "Maybe we could go out right after breakfast."

They had no sooner dressed, when Olga knocked on the door and brought them their breakfast on a tray.

"Everyone sleeps late after a big party like last night's, but I thought you young ladies would probably want something to eat now," Olga said, smiling. She put the tray on a round table in their sitting room, and began unloading the dishes.

"But you have four place settings, and there are only two of us," Mandie remarked.

"Nein, there will soon be four of you," the maid said.

"Miss Dorothy said she would like to eat with you, and also your friend, Mister Jonathan."

At her remark, Dorothy and Jonathan both appeared in the open doorway.

"Come in," Mandie invited. "You two are up early. Olga has brought us a delicious breakfast."

Jonathan and Dorothy greeted the girls and sat down at the table.

"Celia and I want to go outside and watch that juniper tree when we're finished eating. We're supposed to leave here tomorrow, I think, so we don't have much time left," Mandie remarked as Olga poured the hot tea.

"I wish you luck," Olga said. "I have never seen the tree jump myself, and I doubt it really happens."

"Maybe we'll be fortunate enough to see it," Dorothy said as she buttered a hot roll.

Olga smiled at Dorothy and said, "If there is nothing else, I will see if others would like breakfast in their rooms."

"Oh, yes, thank you, Olga," Mandie told her. "It was really nice of you to think of us."

Olga started out the door and turned back to say, "You Americans are so polite and friendly. Good day now." She went out, leaving the door open.

As soon as the four young people had eaten all they could, Mandie fed Snowball the scraps. Then she put his harness and leash on him and they all went outside.

Mandie led the way to the low wall where they sat whenever they watched the tree. It was near the driveway, and just as they started to sit down, a large extravagant carriage came speeding down the driveway toward the road. Mandie caught a glimpse of Elsa and her aunt inside as it passed.

"That was Elsa and her aunt!" Mandie exclaimed. The

others nodded. "So they're leaving. I wonder why? I thought they were going to stay a few days. They just arrived night before last," she remarked.

"Look!" Jonathan said, pointing to two riders in the distance. "That may be the reason why."

"It's Rupert and Lady Catherine!" Mandie exclaimed.

"Looks like his engagement has been broken," Celia said.

"And all for the good," Dorothy added. "I'm not really fond of Elsa, but she deserves a better husband than Rupert would be."

"I wonder what happened?" Mandie asked.

"My father told me part of what happened," Dorothy offered. "Elsa's aunt was upset by the appearance of Lady Catherine last night, because everyone knows the lady has been after Rupert. And most people knew Rupert didn't want to marry Elsa. So when the baroness was polite to Catherine, rather than asking her to leave as everyone expected her to do, the aunt became furious."

"Well, at least one wrong has been righted," Mandie said. "And we have solved some of the mysteries surrounding this place, but this tree is determined not to allow us to see it jump."

"The rain is not going to allow it either," Jonathan quickly added as a sudden downpour sent them all running to the castle for protection. They stood inside the front hallway, waiting to see if the rain would stop, but from there they couldn't see the juniper tree.

The rain lasted so long, they began to wander around inside the castle. But no one else seemed to be up and about except the servants. Finally the heavy deluge stopped.

"It has stopped raining," Mandie observed, looking out a window in the library where they had gone. "Shall we go back outside?"

The others agreed, and they found their way to the front door and around to the end where the tree stood. Just as they rounded the corner, all four of them stopped and gasped in wonder. The juniper tree was actually jumping up and down! They could see the tree actually making jerky little jumps.

In all the excitement, Mandie set Snowball down, forgetting to fasten on his leash, which she had removed while they were in the house. The white kitten headed toward the tree, and Mandie tried to catch him, while her friends stood frozen in excitement.

Snowball led Mandie on a chase, and stopped at the opening of a huge drainpipe that seemed in some way connected to the moat. Though the rain had stopped, an intermittent flow of water still came out of the pipe, and Snowball pawed at the debris floating along.

When Mandie reached down to pick him up, he looked at her playfully and darted inside the enormous pipe. Mandie sighed in exasperation when she couldn't reach him. Her friends were out of sight around the corner of the castle.

"Snowball, you come here!" she called to the kitten.

Snowball meowed from inside the pipe and refused to come out. Mandie tucked the end of her long skirt up into the waistband and stooped way down to crawl into the pipe. She could feel the flowing water, moving in waves as if it were being pumped out of the pipe. Her shoes plowed mud as she moved inward, and Snowball ran still deeper into the tunnel when Mandie approached him.

"Snowball, Snowball! Kitty, kitty, come here!" she called, but he wouldn't come near enough for her to grab him.

Mandie was far enough inside that she could see only

inches in front of her face. Suddenly she bumped into something rough and tangled; the culvert was blocked by something she couldn't identify.

Whatever it was, it was moving and felt scary, even dangerous. Her heart began to pound.

She couldn't see for sure, but she was afraid Snowball had somehow been trapped by this thing, for she heard Snowball's meow close by, but could not see the kitty.

As much as she cared for her kitten, Mandie was scared. She turned to go back, but the pipe was too small to allow her to turn. She could only move backward—and that she did as quickly as she was able, bent to the floor of the pipe.

Snowball still crouched deep inside watching her.

Mandie backed out the opening where she had gone in, and straightened up. She was dirty and wet. Her grandmother would have a fit if she saw her in such condition. She thought she'd better slip up to her room and change clothes.

Mandie reached the corner where she'd left her friends, and found them still watching in awe as the juniper tree jumped up and down.

"I've got to go change clothes," she called to them. "And I want Uncle Ned to see the tree moving."

"Here comes Uncle Ned now," Jonathan answered, pointing toward the pathway from around the castle.

Mandie ran to meet him. Uncle Ned looked surprised at her appearance, but before he could speak she took him by the hand and practically dragged him to see the jumping tree. The old Cherokee stood before it in disbelief.

Suddenly the tree stopped moving. Everyone looked at one another. "What made it do that?" Mandie asked.

"Do not know, Papoose. Never see this happen before," Uncle Ned told her.

"If you all will wait for me, I've got to change my clothes before Grandmother sees me," Mandie said. "Snowball is inside that huge pipe around the corner. That's where I got so wet and dirty. He won't come out. And, Uncle Ned, there is something strange and scary inside the pipe, something moving. I was terrified—it felt almost like some snakes or something awful like that."

"Where, Papoose?" Uncle Ned asked.

"Here, I'll show you." Mandie led the way and the others followed. She stooped down and pointed inside. "Snowball's in there."

Uncle Ned stooped to explore the pipe. The water had stopped flowing, so Snowball began to make his way out.

"I see Papoose's white kitten. I see, too, something dark in pipe," he said. He skillfully worked his way into the pipe, and in a few moments he backed out, bringing the wet, dirty kitten with him. With him came a fresh flow of water from the culvert.

When he straightened up, he explained what he'd found in the pipe. "Those not snakes, Papoose. They are roots of juniper tree. When rain swells from underneath, water pushes roots, make big tree jump."

All three young people stared at Uncle Ned in amazement.

"And all the time people here have been thinking there was something mysterious about the tree," Mandie said. "Wait till they hear we've solved the mystery!" She took her kitten from Uncle Ned.

"They are really going to be surprised," Celia remarked.

"Papoose, change clothes," Uncle Ned told her. "Then we talk about tree."

"Yes, I've got to clean up," she told her friends. "I'll be right back." She turned and hurried toward the castle with the kitten in her arms.

"It's all your fault, Snowball," she said. He meowed in response. "But then, I guess if you hadn't entered the drainpipe we wouldn't have discovered how the juniper jumped."

Mandie entered the hallway and crept along quietly, looking around in hopes no one would see her. There didn't seem to be anyone anywhere, not even the servants.

In her room she quickly cleaned up, and changed her dress and shoes. She washed Snowball too, and tried to rub him dry.

"Oh, Snowball, I can't get you dry. You're going to have to go back outside and dry. I can't leave you on our bed all wet like this," she told him.

Letting Snowball walk on his leash, Mandie hurried back down the stairs and outside to look for her friends. When she rounded the corner toward the juniper tree, no one was in sight. She ran to look at the stream that went through the pipeline and saw that it was very low now. The force of the water was gone.

"Well, where did everybody go?" she said to herself as she walked around. She didn't see a single soul anywhere.

"Maybe they went down the pathway for a walk," she told herself. She quickly followed the pathway and let Snowball walk on his leash. He kept cutting flips and playing along the way.

As she came to an intersection in the pathway she stopped to listen. Was that the sound of a horse nearby? She jumped behind a huge tree just as Rupert raced by on his horse. He didn't see her, but Snowball had managed to pull loose from his leash and the horse had scared him away.

Mandie ran after him down the pathway. She kept

calling to him, but he wouldn't even stop and look back at her. Finally she came into a clearing and she knew the lake would be just ahead in the stand of trees.

"Snowball! Come here!" she called to the white kitten.

Every time she called him he seemed to run that much faster. She tried to run faster herself, and when she got near the lake, which was just beyond a steep incline, she lost her footing and started to slide.

"Oh, goodness!" she gasped as she slipped on the loose pebbles and suddenly went over the edge and into the water.

"Help!" she cried. "I can't swim!"

She fought to stay on top of the water and tried to push herself back toward the shore, but the water seemed to have a mind of its own, and she knew she would drown if something or someone didn't save her.

Lifting her head as far as she could out of the swirling water, she cried out, "What time I am afraid I will put my trust in Thee. Dear Lord, please save me."

Snowball was wildly meowing in the distance as she sank into the dark depths of the water. Sudden sharp pains in her chest cut off her breath. Her long skirts, heavy with water, pulled her toward the bottom of the lake.

I am dying. What will my mother ever do? was her last thought.

Suddenly something was pulling at her hair. Oh, it hurt! Then whatever it was attached itself to the wet folds of her skirt and pulled. A hand rubbed across her face and she was violently thrown about. This was too much to fight. She gave up.

"Papoose, Papoose," Uncle Ned was calling her.

Able to finally force her eyelids open, she looked up into the worried face of her old Cherokee friend while he cradled her in his arms on the shore of the lake.

She couldn't speak as she felt herself being lifted and placed on a hard flat surface. She realized she was in the pony cart as she and Uncle Ned began moving.

The Lord had answered her plea. *Thank you, dear, Lord,* she thought.

After frenzied care at the castle, Mandie was finally able to be propped up on pillows. Uncle Ned sat by her side. She noticed Rupert standing in the background.

"Thank you, Uncle Ned," she managed to say between violent coughs. "You always come to my rescue."

"No, no, Papoose," Uncle Ned told her as he held her hand. "Not Ned. Rupert got Papoose out of lake. Ned come later."

"Rupert!" Mandie weakly repeated as she turned her head to look at the baroness's grandson. Rupert quickly avoided her look and hurried out through the doorway.

"I'll thank him later," Mandie said.